LOVE
and Marriage
for A Lifetime

TWO BOOKS IN ONE. LET THE JOURNEY BEGIN.

Love (Vol. I)

Marriage (Vol.II)

DR. DAVID R.L. STEVENS

5830 E 2nd St, Ste 7000 #9983
Casper, WY 82609
USA

CONTENTS

LOVE and Marriage for A Lifetime

Two books in one. Let the journey begin.

LOVE Volume 1

Foreword ix

Chapter 1: Dating, The First Measure.. 1

Chapter 2: Dating - The Ins and The Outs. 9

Chapter 3: Dating, Looking At Our Backgrounds . .. .25

Chapter 4: Should We Date, Get Engaged Or End It? . .. .31

Chapter 5: The Leaving Factor. 39

Chapter 6: More About Leaving . .. .56

Chapter 7: The Cleaving Factor 62

Chapter 8: Grease-Paint and Ceremony.. 68

LOVE and Marriage for A Lifetime

Two books in one. Let the journey continue.

MARRIAGE Volume 2

Chapter 1: After You Say I Do 91

Chapter 2: Different Strokes . .. .110

Chapter 3:   But You Are So Different. 125
Chapter 4:   Your Wife Wants You To Know 134
Chapter 5:   Husbands And Their Secrets.. 144
Chapter 6:   Ready, Set, Go! What's The Plan? 154
Chapter 7:   Who's In Charge . .. .169
Chapter 8:   Essential Partnering 189

LOVE AND MARRIAGE FOR A LIFETIME

**Two books in one.
Let the journey begin. LOVE Volume 1**

DEDICATION

I dedicate this special two volume work to God and His church, and then of course, to my beautiful wife Dorothy who has been my rock and special angel for more than sixty years. Special recognition to our four children and their spouses, Mike & Becky, Shana, still my editor extraordinaire & Brian, Faith & Russell, and David & Robin, who are all involved in kingdom work. Now you know I'm not going to leave out our ten grandchildren, by age: Michael, Timothy, Daniel, Joshua, Imani, Sarah, David Kweli, Nyla, Nia, and Solomon Kabisa. Also, this is the first book that I get to introduce our two great grands, Christian and Fawn. What a wonderful growing dynasty in the making! Thank you, Christ Center Church of God, for sharing us with the world at large. You've allowed us to go and serve others in seminars and workshops without complaint. In those times when I needed time to write, you were most gracious, even when we took a partial sabbatical that was not on anyone's radar. I am truly blessed to have such a great congregation of loving, caring people. Thank you again for not placing too many extra demands on our time. You have grasped the understanding that God has not only sent us to serve you, but a larger world as well; and we love you with our lives! Then there is my special staff: Pastors Elsa Johnson Bass, and Vera H. Odum, Brian Boykin, David Scott Owens III., Cornelius Bolger, who with my Administrative Assistant Ms. Beverly J.

Adams, continue to make me look good. Thank you so much for all of your dedicated work.

May God continue to bless you and your families as you serve the Kingdom.

"Rev"

FOREWORD

This is book one of this combined volume series on growing in a relationship. We concentrate here on falling in love the right way and being able to build a stable relationship that will stand the test of life. The reader will notice in this work that the dating process is foundational to what can follow. Whether the experience leads to courtship or breaking up, you will find us there sharing gems of wisdom. We talk about love and engagement, and even the wedding ceremony.

I've tried to pull out from the Bible the wisdom that continues to help anyone wise enough to seek it. I have included many real- life accounts that help bring focus to principles. For it is in following principles that we gain the highest and richest blessings from God.

Judge Joan Barnes Perry-Stewart said, *"Everybody needs this information! Smart, not so smart, singles, couples . . . EVERYBODY"!* We do agree, and hope that singles, divorced, and married folks read this collection of wisdom gleaned from the wisdom that The Marriage Maker provides. We also recommend that where possible, couples and spouses read, study, and discuss these chapters together. You will find this series of books helpful in all kinds of discussion groups.

Our first four books, *MARRIAGE: The Corridors, Castles, and Conflicts; MARRIAGE: The Rules of the Game; MARRIAGE: Catching A Second Wind; and xxx LOVE, MARRIAGE, and THE BABY CARRIAGE* can be used as textbooks in the classroom. We believe that biblical principles always work. However, because of one's culture and tradition and maybe sometimes a particular lifestyle, some principles are more adaptable than others, or it may take a longer time to understand the application. Remember, however, some flexibility does not mean avoiding, ignoring, or rejecting a principle.

Please enjoy this latest effort; it is intended to be simple and easy to understand, yet yielding an impactful surge in your relationship energy. Knowledge is power. Power to understand, and power to activate that understanding. Practicing these truths will lead to a greater life. Once again, *I give to you almost fifty years of experience and passionate study.*

CHAPTER 1

DATING, THE FIRST MEASURE

Genesis 2:18

And the Lord God said, "It is not good that man (the male)
should be alone: I will make him a help (fitted) for him."

WHEN A GREAT house is built, a great deal of work goes on down
underground. A foundation is laid, sometimes a basement is dug, and a
lot of money is spent before the great structure even reaches street level.
Interestingly enough in today's market, if we can think of marriage as
a great house, we see often that there is little or no preparation being
placed beneath the first floor. Christ was concerned about foundation
in His reference to the two houses being built (Mat.7:24-27). One was
foolishly built on sand. Sand in and of itself is not known for its building
stability. The other house was built on a rock foundation. Because of the
stable properties of rock anything anchored to it, and in it, will stand!

So it is that I propose that we consider dating foundational to marriage. It is highly unlikely that one will marry someone that he or she has not dated, especially in this day. Yet so little of this important social function is really understood. So,, the first measure of the future of a relationship begins with dating. We can almost say, *"How goes the date is how goes the relationship"*. But now it would be a bit unfair to judge on one single date alone. But it does not take a significant number of these dates to tell either.

At the risk of sounding rather blunt and fanatical let me say that **you should not date a person that you would not marry**. I'm sure you have heard that old expression, "I wouldn't marry that person if they were the last person on earth." Sounds good, but I'm not sure if that is altogether true. Dating should not be practiced as a casual meaningless function. It can be a very careless act when it is done only to fill in lonely hours of boredom. Yet many times it is thought of in just that way. A boredom replacement. Something to do to fill the time.

We recognize that there is an element within the dating borders that is useful in pushing back loneliness. But be very careful about why you are seeking someone else's company. Desperation, boredom, and social frustration may cause participants to make hasty decisions. Decisions that may affect a lifetime of negative results. Laura a divorcee, had been lonely and free from that relationship for several years. She kept meeting men who would date her but had no intentions of marrying her. These men she met found her attractive but really were looking more for a good bed partner. She wanted so desperately to be married again that she allowed herself to be fooled time after time. She set aside her Christian principles because she thought that her indiscretions would be justified when she got the ring and the ceremony. Somebody's Grand Mom said, *"Why buy the cow if you can get the milk free"*? Many lonely women make this same desperate mistake. We know on the positive end of careful dating that boredom and loneliness, especially for mature adults, can be replaced with healthy excitement. Sometimes this excitement will turn into love and marriage. But give the process time and careful observation.

Dating is like window-shopping. It should be seen as the testing ground for a possible great house to come. Please understand, I'm not expecting two seventeen -year old daters to go out with the expectation that their dates are the beginning of a whirlwind courtship in which they will get married to each other within four or five years. What I do expect is that these young people will use that time together, whether one time, or many times, to find out the important things about each other. I think it is the same for more mature adults who may feel to take less time in making a life decision. I'm not so sure however that I recommend any age group rushing to a relationship decision.

Please further understand when I make the outlandish statement not to date someone you would not marry I do not expect someone to date only one individual in life with the ultimate purpose of marrying that one person. In fact, I believe that one should choose a marriage partner after having dated many worthy persons. What I am talking about is really a respect for time and the things that your inner senses are telling you.

Don't date the kind of individual that you can't respect. Why spend time with someone you have already determined is a washout? Then secondly don't disregard those little voices that are speaking in your head. The reason I am so adamant on these points is that I believe we have the ability to fall in love with just about anybody. Later on, we will qualify the term love, but for now, let's just say generally, "love".

There are many individuals floating around on polluted clouds, mistakenly thinking that it indicates that one has some special chemistry to fall in love. I doubt that Cupid goes about sending love laden arrows into the hearts of would-be prospects. Because one falls in love is not an indicator that it is a potential marriage made in heaven. If this were true according to today's statistics, heaven had better check its computers because a lot of its work is headed for the shredder. I happen to believe that God does not make mistakes, but people make mistakes when they misapply data in favor of personal whims. If you are thrown into a constant social situation that lends itself to the romantic, it takes no special chemistry to fall deeply in love.

Put two single individuals, a male, and a female, who are very much unlike each other on a deserted island together. At first, they may not even like each other but give it enough time. If the rescue is greatly delayed, you will see them drawing closer and closer toward each other. All their old cautions and objections will fade with time. They will begin to just settle because their field has narrowed.

Earl and Tammy lived in the same neighborhood as youngsters. They went to the same small church. Constantly they found themselves in the same groups. In high school it just seemed natural for them to date each other eventually leading to a commitment. Under circumstances a little less pressured Tammy would not have chosen Earl as a husband. She knew what he was like—yet there was a growing interest. Once, when they were going steady, in a jealous rage, he swung at her with a stick just narrowly missing her. Tammy was outraged and broke off the relationship. Later Earl began to show her every reason why she should reconsider being his wife. They never mentioned the event that caused them to break up. He never asked for forgiveness, and she felt too uneasy to bring it up. Alarmingly before they got married there were seeds of mistrust, hidden anger, and faulty communication planted. Tammy at this point was not listening to her head or some of her friends. Because her heart pounded with excitement when he was near she took this as a sign of a guaranteed future. She should have been paying attention to some other signs however. He showed no interest in school, had no hobbies and had few if any friends. All of these were important indications of the kind of man she was dealing with. She just settled!

Tammy planned to make it in life as a businesswoman. Earl's biggest plan was to get a job and buy a fancy sports car. He had no great ambition, but because she was full of ambitions she overlooked his lack thereof. She was an active Christian yet there were those times when she doubted his relationship to the Lord. She never seemed to know where he was coming from spiritually but again she passed over it. She was warned during the dating period by friends not to continue in this hopeless relationship. Their: family background, their educational goals, their spiritual goals all were completely different from each other. Of course, there were a few people who thought that they would make a cute couple. Eventually against her better judgment and the voices of some close friends she married him anyway. For Earl she represented comfort and beauty. He was dazzled by her and that was good enough for him.

I've heard that a steady drop of water will wear away stone. Here it seems to be true. I don't know, perhaps it was out of Tammy's need to belong to someone. Maybe she felt that no one else would come along. We are not sure, what pushed her over the threshold. Predictably their marriage has been a real up and down trial. What once was love, is now barely tolerance! Both, after several years, wish they could terminate the relationship. Tammy regrets not having a husband that she can feel secure with, and regrets that even her children suffer because of a weak father. Earl on the other hand is not really a bad person. He is mostly confused by his role as father/husband. He feels pressured by his wife who wants him to measure up. He does not know how to measure up. He never had a father figure at all! His whole world has been, narrow and limited. Tammy's interest in theater, museums, and travel bore him to tears. Why can't she just be satisfied to stay home and watch wrestling, boxing, and soap operas? They have almost no friends, certainly no close ones, because Earl doesn't like people. He does not want to be bothered by his family, or hers. Tammy has now taken up the sport of nagging. Nagging about anything, and everything! Their lack of tolerance has now escalated into a physical thing. Pushing and shoving has now been added to their acceptance. There are three children who suffer in this relationship. Let the reader understand, the problems this young couple are experiencing are really not the result of the years they've been married, but rather they result from the days they started to date each other. The signs for failure were there all along but ignored. A young man in our church engaged me in a conversation that fits here. He asked me if I remembered a young lady that came to church with him a few weeks before? *"Rev., wow was she a good actress. She really fooled me!"* He explained his bewilderment of almost getting hooked on a girl who seemed like she was right in line with what he felt about life, the church, and the Lord. *"Rev,"* he said, *"she told me she was a Christian and I believed her. But after her visit to church I saw her talking to another guy while displaying a completely different character. The very next time I saw her she was playing up to another dude, showing that same unchristian side."* My young friend had been temporarily crushed. Had he been foolish enough to base a whole involvement of his emotions on that first date, he would have been in real trouble. Even though hurt by this discovery that the young lady was a double agent, it did not destroy him! He was blessed because he took a second look and acted according to the total information.

Many people involved in dating rarely take a second look at the situation! Then there are perhaps an even smaller number of these folks who actually, pay serious attention to the negative findings. Dating is a time of information gathering. A time of storing just like we input into a computer bank awaiting a conclusion based on that same gathered information. Claude and Belinda were about as different as chalk and cheese. Claude was a rather shy and homey man who was much older than Bell. He had been married many years before and had had a string of broken relationships following his divorce. In each of these relationships the women ended up taking him to the cleaners. The general pattern was that he would come home one day and find the furniture gone.

Bell was very attractive, outgoing, but also designing. Maybe adding the word *stealth,* might help the reader to get the picture. She had also been a product of a divorce. Add to all the other characteristics that she had the word *ambition.* Bell was going to be somebody special! She felt herself to be a rising star in the wings. She planned to have it all her way. In another chapter we will look more in depth at their marriage. But for now, let's stick to a few basic observations. Claude was a very lonely man, hurt by a cruel past of betrayals. He was very plain on the outside, but inside he had a heart of gold—just waiting to be given away. Belinda could see past the fake front that he had erected to protect the tender character couching inside.

Her plan was simple. She overwhelmed him with attention and what seemed like love. She so adequately met every need he had. She literally poured the love on! He thought at long last he had been successful in winning the attention of a beautiful woman who was giving to him all of what he felt he needed in life.

In conversations with him during their engagement, I found that even though his heart seemed to be firmly settled on, 'Lovers Row', there were many indicators that all was not settled on 'Thinkers Island'. Yes, the indicators for failure were all really there. Their purposes for dating were at odds from the beginning. He wanted a Trophy Wife who would love him, and she wanted a Sugar Daddy who would support her.

Now it might seem as if I am slapping at Bell for her dishonesty. That I am, but listen, Claude was dishonest also. Both were selfish. He was lonely and sought to erase it by allowing her to shower him with affection. He gave in to her every whim without once putting his foot down. He made her feel that her actions of selfishness were acceptable." Just keep pouring on the love and everything goes!" Bell only fed his hunger because it fit well into her design for future gold. She confessed later that she never loved him. She used him to move away from the bottom of life after her divorce. Claude and his money could support her life style changes.

I've shared this account to make a few simple points about the importance of dating, especially, but not exclusively, to those beyond their' teenage years.

1. *Know your motives for dating, making sure they are honest and forthright*
2. *Evaluate honestly the other person's motives for dating. (you need to know them as much as possible)*
3. *Share honestly your motives and expect the other person to do so.*
4. *Evaluate as you go along in this relationship, openly sharing the findings.*
5. *During the dating period, and any time prior to marriage; be open to relationship termination.*

What benefit is there to making the unworkable—workable? Is there some kind of prize at the end of the rainbow? I think not! Sometimes there are those who feel under pressure to continue dating someone who is not really their choice. Sometimes its peer pressure, or family pressure, or often just pure ego. Whatever the reason, if it won't work, it won't work! There is no shame in terminating a courtship or even an engagement that is destined to go nowhere. Claude closed his eyes to Belinda's behavior and pretended that it would not spoil their relationship. They insisted on getting married. It did not work!

CHAPTER 2

DATING - THE INS AND THE OUTS

Song of Solomon 2:4,5 & 8 (N.A.S.)

*"HE has brought me to his banquet hall, and his banner is love.
"Sustain me with raisin cakes; refresh me with apples, because I
am lovesick. "Listen, my beloved! Behold, he is coming, climbing
on the mountains, leaping on the hills!*

IN CHAPTER ONE, we went to great lengths to express just how important the date is in the building of a relationship. It was seen as a foundation stone. In this chapter I would like to offer further help. This time, we will consider the make-up of the date: the types of dates, and some possible places to go on dates.

There is a scene in the play, "Better Than Sacrifice," by Elsa Johnson-Bass, that finds a young tough named Troy at the wheel of his car. He has just picked up Kim, a rather confused, rebellious teen, who sits tightly at his side. The audience is to discover that they really don't know each other well, but Troy is on the make and Kim just wants to get away from the watchful eyes of her older brother, and his wife. She and a younger sister have moved in with them after the sudden death of their parents. Kim has become so blinded by her hatred for losing her parents that she hardly cares what happens to her. Troy is not interested in what her reasons are for taking him up on his offer to go joy riding. He has his own plans! The first date was "checking out time". This girl could be a star in his production. In a later scene, we find Kim crying her eyes out while waiting for her folks to come and get her out of jail. It seems that on their second car date, Troy pulled into a Seven/Eleven store to get something. Kim, unaware of what was taking place, sat there waiting for him to return. The next thing she knew, flashing police lights accompanied the blaring shrill of sirens, and the screeching of tires. Troy had tried unsuccessfully to stick up the storeowner. Being the gentleman that he was, he thought it proper to involve Kim as an accomplice. Later after she had been arrested, and humiliated, he changed his story.

Aimless dates that go nowhere are usually not a good idea. Kim foolishly accepted the invitation to go joy riding without giving very much thought to how it would end up. I see this thoughtlessness as an open invitation to trouble. Successful dating results from good planning. I don't suggest that this episode is typical. I realize that I am beginning with a rather way out example, but my point is that aimless dating can lead anywhere, or nowhere. It reminds me of the illustration of two old farmers having target practice one day. The first farmer felt rather good when he picked off about eight out of ten cans sitting on the fence with his riffle. The two he missed, at least he knew they were clear misses. The second farmer took aim with a scattergun. When he let go, everything went; fence, cans and all. He never knew if he blew the fence out beneath the cans, or in spite of the cans. If you aim at nothing the results are rather speculative. Or on the other hand as someone else said, *"If you aim at nothing you'll hit it every time."* If a date is to be successful, a lot of planning ought to go into it. People often get into trouble when they don't know where they are going, when they are going to get there, how long they're going to stay, and when they'll return. When my daughter is going out on a date, as her father, I want to know whom, when, where, for what reason, and for how long! I don't feel that this is unreasonable. These are questions that she has to have answers for herself. I'm just the reinforcement element. For your own safety and protection, say where you are going and go where you say. This is a practice that I observe even to this day. My family ought to be able to trace my where bouts with little difficulty. If a change in plans occurs, a phone call can update your location and adjusted plans. This is not bondage my friend, rather it is freedom.

James and Joan were very much in love when in college. They were beyond the formal date where there has to be a purpose, a place and a time, etc. Their main purpose was usually just to be together. James had a fancy sports car-that usually supplied the place. The problem of them wandering around from one lovers' spot to another was often highlighted by the frequent break down of James' sports car. He often had to make a late hour call, for his friend in the dorm to come and pull, or push them out of some out of the way place that probably would not show up on a map. James was a master of the clandestine. Imagine being about a mile or two outside of the suburbs of a city, another mile or so from a back road, onto a tractor path that leads to the back of some farmer's field. Yep, you got it! That was their normal kind of place.

Now even though both confessed to be born again, it is hard to visualize much prayer and Bible study going on. Probably the most dramatic moments took place when James' father and mother showed up one night at the dorm. They had come from home, two states away, unannounced, and were anxious to see their son. The guys in the dorm were amazed at the timing as they tried to think up a reasonable explanation to cover for James. James had just ten minutes before stumbled into the dorm half frost bitten and out of breath announcing a need for help. His car had once again failed to start, leaving them stranded.

This time it was in another direction of town. Actually it turned out to be the city dump. After giving hurried directions to his friend, he again stumbled into the night half crazed by his obvious running in the freezing weather.

Now in the midst of getting dressed and putting on their coats to go bail out their friends from this latest trouble, more trouble comes. What do you say to anxious parents to not alarm them when you are alarmed? The boys explained that they were just on their way to get James (no mention of Joan) who had a little trouble starting his car. The parents were told that they could make themselves comfortable until the fellows returned. What parents are going to really go for that? They insisted on following in their car. Wow was this some real trouble. The boys knew that Joan was with James. How were they going to get a message to them before Mom, and Dad arrived on the scene?

The boys gave vague directions to the parents hoping they would get lost. This was a good possibility since they were not quite sure how to find this place themselves. Since the boys only had one car, the plan was to drive near enough to the spot, drop off one of the guys who could run the rest of the way, alert the unsuspecting couple and then somehow blend in with the arrival of the cars.

The timing was perfect. Phil got out unnoticed at the corner and headed for what seemed like the spot. Just as he disappeared in the darkness and the car pulled off again, the parents caught up. The boys slowly pulled through a few unnecessary streets hoping to burn up some more time. It was amazing that when they turned one of those corners Phil hopped in again, without the parents seeing him. They finally pulled off the main road onto a winding strip that led to the city dump. Off to the side was the stalled car. The guys pulled up in back of the car to push it. The problem for the friends was that Dad was out of his car so fast that they could not talk to James, and Joan was missing. In just a brief slurred sentence James managed to whisper, "Come back for Joan." It was so quickly said that it was only God's mercy that it was heard at all.

The car was pushed out eventually starting and all three cars were on their way back to the dorm. The trick was how was the second car with the friends in it going to drop out and double back. Somehow, they made up some excuse continuing on as the others turned for the dorm. The friends faithfully turned back to look for Joan. They were not sure if they had heard the message right, or just where to look for her. They returned to where the car had stalled and got out on foot. They called her name hoping that she was close. It was so cold that they began to fear for her safety. In front of them a pile of leaves and twigs began to move. Slowly, Joan began to crawl out from the hasty shelter. Shaking violently from the cold, she sobbed softly. Nothing was said in the ride home, but in every mind there was a torrid of words. But overriding it all was, "Thank God, Joan has been found"!

Joan and James felt all along that it was their business what they did. They could set their own purpose, their own time, and their own place. It was up to them, they thought. Yet as we have seen, that was not true. Look how many people were involved in the Big Cover up! How much Christian growth was actually experienced by either of these young people? Had a *reasonable* purpose or goal been established at the very beginning of each date they would have had some direction and ability to measure the success of that goal. An example might be, "There's a play tonight at the Campus Theater. It begins at 7:00 P.M. So, I'll pick you up at 6:30 P.M. The play should be over at about 10:00 P.M. and we could go from there to the Local pizza- place. I should be able to have you home by 11: 00 or 11: 30 at the latest." Here we have purpose, time, place, and termination time. Our system is now measurable. James arrives at 6:30 as planned. They go to the play as planned. The play lets out fifteen minutes early so they can go to get pizza early, thus getting in fifteen minutes before *deadline.* Now why would I call it a dead line? Well if you consciously make an agreed upon schedule, it becomes a type of contract. When you say, "Back no later than," that means no later than! In all of your planning, be honest. Don't plan a lot of messing around time. That could really prove to be messy. Once your plan has been set, *tell someone!*

One of the mistakes James and Joan made, among others, was that they set themselves up so that they were answerable to no one. Now it is true that they were grown, but it is beneficial for everyone to be in subjection to someone or some group that represents positive values. The Bible teaches us a system of subjection. It talks of being under the authority of the church. It talks of the church being under the authority of Christ. Even the animals are placed under the dominion of man. Then everything is under God, Elohim—He who creates and makes covenants swearing by Himself. Friend, that's a real system of authority.

There are some secular songs that could speak well to us at this point. One writer suggests that "No man is an island; no man stands alone . . ." Then there's that instructive warning, "Everybody needs somebody sometime"! Building a protective moral support system is important. If you use it, it will provide a type of freedom. Fail to use it and you have little to back you up.

Parents always are a good first line resource. When you know that plans have been set it is a good idea to share that information with them. If you do not have parents, or they are too far away to be effective, then find a good friend, or a relative, or, if need be, a reliable neighbor. Give to them as much detail as you can about your plans for the evening. Information like the name and address of your date, where you are going, the various time expectations, and again that, "Home at the latest," time.

I can hear some folks who are older saying they don't need to plug into such a young person's system. These folks may feel that they are too mature for this, but trouble has no age limit. It will not hurt you, not even your pride to take a few minutes to share your plans with someone else who will care. Those extra efforts are for your safety and your back up.

This advice is for young and mature single men as well as young and mature single ladies. Do you recall the story of Joseph in the Bible?

(Genesis 39.) Well Joseph entered into the master's house, who was away at the time, to attend to some business. The master's wife was not a nice lady! She tried to force Joseph to bed with her but he ran out. Well he ran, but she snatched his coat. Joseph was an upright lad, but without a backup who could verify his actions? He was, as they say, "Up a creek without a paddle." Maybe a reliable witness would have made a difference, maybe not. It turned out so strangely that I don't believe that the master believed his wife either, but he had to go along with her report as much as he could. We see that Joseph got a prison sentence rather than the usual punishment of being put to death.

One other thing I'd like to suggest. Let your date know at the very beginning that you've given the information about your date to someone else. This sometimes eases the pressure before it has a chance to build. There is absolutely nothing wrong with a little more self-protection. When your dating partner knows that someone else knows of your where bouts it will tend to help motivate them into trying to make that date a delightful occasion. Automatically one knows that if someone else has been informed concerning the date, and all of its' expected details, the very first thing that other party is going to ask afterward is, "How did it go"?

MORE ABOUT MAKING THE DATE

Webster's dictionary defines a date as a social engagement between persons of the opposite sex. That's about as exciting sounding as two mailmen meeting on a corner to exchange mailbags. It is a social engagement and usually between two individuals of the opposite sex, but it can be so much more. Missing from the Webster definition are words like, pleasurable, enjoyable, and instructive. There is no hint of having emotional interest and value.

Where you go has to be as important as the going. The place you choose could affect the way the date goes. A fellow who wants to find out what's in a girls' mind will take her to a place of conversation. Meeting for dinner or lunch is always a good idea. Maybe because of our schedules, or patterns of living, breakfast dates have often been overlooked. Yet I think that it makes for a rather romantic idea if it can be worked out. My wife reminded me of the library date. Here you have to talk in hushed tones. This kind of quiet atmosphere might cause some people to go kind of nuts. You need to know this about the person you are dating, but to others it can be fun studying together.

Walking dates also help set the stage for conversation. Try walking together in several different environments. A nature walking date through the park or on a country road can produce the kind of conversation that tells how a person views the creations of God. The hope here is that the date won't go trying to step on every bug and swat every bee buzzing. It provides the kind of backdrop to help us explore just how we line up with God's will, and His purpose for our lives. It helps the dreamer in us loosen up.

Then there is the walking date through a shopping area. You can learn a lot about a person as you see them negotiate a crowd of strange people. What attitudes come out as they are jostled and pushed about? Can they cope? Are they still able to conduct business, or must they retreat to quiet safety to survive? If this kind of date is planned to actually do some shopping, it might give you some ideas of how the other person handles money. Now I know that it all sounds stuffy like business, but if planned well, it can be a lot of fun!

There is some history in just about every place. Walking about viewing history through the architecture of your city, town or area might prove of interest to some. If you are blessed to live in an area that has a museum then you ought to take advantage of it. A good walking activity for a large group of daters is a park-trail hike. I recommend that this sort of thing be done in groups because of the safety factor.

I believe group dating to be one of the most beneficial kinds of events.

Much depends; of course, on the group you choose to be with. If you do not select the other persons carefully, it could have just as much potential for harm. I know of a couple who decided to go to a drive-in movie with another couple. The other couple was into some pretty heavy necking and petting. This began to affect the more innocent daters. They too began to explore, and experiment with this new- found freedom to the point that their behavior exceeded their mentors. Afterward, I'm sure what followed was shame and embarrassment. They had blown "their cool"! In today's language, they had not gone "all the way", but they had managed to reveal a definite weakness—a lack of self-control. Then the other problem is that once certain plateaus have been reached it is hard to be satisfied with lesser expressions. Only the power of God could give the strength to retreat.

Only the Spirit of God would even cause one to want to retreat.

However, with that caution of selecting group members carefully, I feel that group dating can be a lot of fun. This kind of dating can delay premature romantic pressures. Many people could really get to know each other if romance would not get in the way." Aha! He's against romance," you say! No not at all. What I'm trying to convey is that romance often comes too early. Before some have had a chance to become good friends, they become lovers! Many persons after reaching that stage never return to developing friendship. They go on rather to develop their romantic goals. I'm afraid that this is the poor stuff that many marriages are made of. When romance fades there's little else to sustain it.

We have talked mostly about less active types of dates. Along with that I should have mentioned, concerts, gallery exhibits, and religious services. Yet now I would like to turn to some more active suggestions. You can learn some things about a person by watching them at a sporting event. Watch out for Mr. Milk-toast who is always super mild and in control; who at a football game turns into a monster shouting death wishes to the opposing team. Perhaps lurking inside that mild exterior is the actual desire to maim, hurt, or break.

I'm reminded of a cousin who told me about the father of a girl that he used to date. It seems that this cousin lived on the far side of New York City. He had to take several busses and trains to go to see this girl. He said he rather enjoyed her company though the travel was long. One night her minister father volunteered to take him home after he had missed the last scheduled train. Since it would keep him from taking a longer route to get home he accepted the ride. After the young couple was seated in the rear of the car, and his wife seated next to him, the good Reverend instructed everybody to "Buckle up!" My cousin thought he saw a strange glint in the Reverend's eye, and was also sure that he had heard a voice change, but he pushed it aside reaching for his girl's hand. He never did quite reach her hand, because the usually mild- mannered parson gunned the engine and took off burning rubber through the streets of New York. It was like the guy behind the wheel had turned into a monster, darting in and out of traffic at unbelievable high speeds. He was like a man possessed until he pulled up to the curb in front of Harold's house. Harold said he was never so glad to see his house. From then on, he politely refused any offers from her father for a ride home. In fact, after that he became quite the expert on train and bus schedules for that area.

The point is that a dater should try to learn as much as can be learned about the person they are dating. This may even include learning something about the family background as well. Observe what you can when your date is being very much in control and when they let their hair down. It is real important to try and find out just who the real person is. Then learn to follow your stronger instincts, also realizing that anyone can have an off day. While much can be learned about your date at spectator sports, it should not be confined to just the watching of others. It is good to find some activities in which you can participate. Everyone can not feel comfortable in active games or sports such as tennis, boating, jogging, skiing, horseback riding, and the like. Then you might consider bowling, roller-skating, or biking. I feel that daters should be placed in some situation where they compete with each other. This can be done even in playing board games such as checkers, or chess, or scrabble. Then there are the games of "Sorry", and "Monopoly", and so many more. A little competition will help you see some character traits in others. I remember my daughter's friend Bobby who could not stand to lose at Monopoly. He turned into someone else right before our eyes. After playing with him for a while you just felt kind of uncomfortable if you were just playing for fun. In another place I saw a family get real-intense when they could not figure out the secrets to some parlor games predicated on secrets. They felt dumped on and took it uncomfortably personal. It was definitely a character flaw.

Returning to activity games for a moment, I'd like to suggest some of the old forgotten ones as interesting dates. Your grandparents probably played some form of shuffleboard. You don't have to have all the fancy paraphernalia. You can improvise. Draw the board out on a piece of flat ground with a piece of chalk. Get two long sticks that you can alter at the bottoms for pushing the disk. Wrap the handle part with some friction tape to protect your hands. Finally find something that is smooth and disc like to be pushed along the surface of the shuffleboard. It should be great fun for the both of you to put your heads together in creating this old game. In high school we used to play a similar game on some old lunch tables. There were three lines [scribed] about two inches apart at both ends of the long table. We would then shoot nickels down the polished surface trying to get the nickel to stop in the last division before the edges of the table. Anything landing in this area between the edge and the first line was worth three points. The next area was two points, and the other area, one point. An exact twenty-one was the goal to win.

Can you imagine the look on your dates' face when you say, *'Let's, play a game of 'Hop Scotch' '*? Why Not? Dates ought to be fun too! Then there's 'Pick Up Sticks', and 'Jacks' and even Marbles, if you're brave. It might even be a good idea to ask some senior citizens about the games that they used to play. This could make for some real interesting future dates. I have shared the above ideas hopefully as springboards toward other ideas. Don't hesitate to develop new and interesting possibilities. The kind of poor planning that has couples ending up in the back seat of a car, panting and pawing each other, or in someone's house unsupervised and uninterrupted, only measures one thing. We want to encourage situations that measure more than the emotional heat level. Arrange for situations that help to identify the inner strengths and qualities. One of the most asked questions (from single eligible young people) is "Where are the boys/men? Where are the girls/women?" It often seems like there's nobody out there. If you happen to be a woman in a church group where there are no eligible men in the local fellowship, don't give up! I am told that there are churches where men are looking for eligible females. The problem of course is to match up congregations and opportunities. I advise pastors and churches to try fellowshipping as much as possible. I know that most congregations are pretty busy at home but if there is a commitment to help single people find life partners, I think time can be found. Churches could jointly plan functions for singles that would provide opportunities for singles to get acquainted. The more congregations joining in such an effort, the wider the appeal.

In addition to in-house programs and joint congregational planning, single people should be encouraged to attend conventions, conferences, camp meetings, and workshops. I further believe that conference planners need to do more creative planning for people to get together in situations where they can meet and learn quality things about each other. So often planners of Christian Youth conventions, singles conventions, and camp meetings, etc. plan only for the "Spiritual man." I offer this caution: when neglecting altogether the social-physical man it tends to strain the spiritual man towards an imbalance. I would compare it to the man, who is not fasting but is just plain hungry for lack of food. You can't tell that man to forget his stomach and concentrate on the Lord. Believe me it is hard to do.

Some individuals have been successful using on-line dating services, but be very careful. There are people out there that use this non- face to face dating method to prey on victims. From what I've been told this is a good method for a lot of people, but everyone says to use caution and common sense. One of the things often mentioned about on-line dating is the ease of fooling someone. I've heard of daters using someone else's pictures. One funny moment seen on television was when two daters showed up at a planned spot but neither was able to recognize the other. Well I think that if a person is ashamed of their appearance enough to lie about it they have already established a character flaw. You are as you are; how could one expect to lie their way into a relationship and then have that relationship turn magically into a wonderful romance. Maybe with our lying couple, because both were deceivers, their act canceled itself out. Still not the most promising scenario.

There are people, sometimes even respected leaders in the local church setting, who tell single people not to even be concerned about finding the right mate. They might say something like, *"When God wants you to have someone, He will send him or her to you. In the mean-time, don't give it a thought."* Now perhaps this sounds spiritual to those impressed by spiritual sounding trivia, but I tend to doubt its effectiveness in helping to quiet the warfare going on inside of some minds. In fact, it is frustrating because the mind/heart feels a need, but other folk reinforce the misconception that if one gets high enough with the Lord, the thought, the need, will all be supernaturally erased. Now if the advice is to not worry about being single, then I agree. Yet being concerned does not in any way suggest over-concern, or worry. I am concerned about tomorrow's dinner. I'm not worried about it. The food must be prepared and served. It must be first removed from the refrigerator, thawed, cleaned, and then cooked. Someone must be available to do this chore. A certain amount of time is needed, and in a busy modern family that too needs to be planned for. Concern here only connotes active scheduling and follow-through. If a single person wants to date hoping to find someone that has a healthy mutual interest in marriage, let's call it exactly that. Worry would not help such persons reach that goal. Good planning, personal availability, and opportunity, all wrapped in prayer is the answer.

In an attempt to explain away not having anyone to date, some Christians simply conclude that it must be God's will for them to remain single. They then paint themselves into a miserable corner—there to stay with a lot of personal disappointment. Folks with this kind of personal disappointment struggle hard against becoming bitter toward God. Jean grew up in the church. She was faithful to her local congregation. In her teen years she dated along with the other young people in their, rather large fellowship. Jean moved out of her teens into the hopeful twenties but no real serious prospects emerged. The fellows she was going out with were not interested in making a life with Jean. Slowly as the years rolled on towards the thirties, Jean decided more and more to become a spiritual giant. She listened to advice to take her mind off the flesh and put it on God. Jean strained to do this. She got even more into church services. Convinced that it must be God's will for her to be alone, she tried hard to "Measure up." I praise God along with her that a certain elderly lady came into her life! This elderly sister gave some sage advice. *"Honey-if the Lord wanted you to be a eunuch for Him, He would not have allowed you to have at the same time that deep longing in your breast to love and be loved by a man. There you are struggling to be free of the very gift that God has given to you. Child, you start asking the Lord right now to give you the desire of your heart. Start thanking Him even before you see the answer."* God in His time, blessed Jean with a great husband and they have now two children.

In case you are not aware, God does answer prayer! This prayer He had to answer in two parts. First, He had to do some work on Jean. She had become tight and very guarded about her emotions. God removed all of that. In Place of all that stuffy self-exile, He brought to her that old softness and self-assuredness she once had. Then God brought along Al.

Al was a handsome young man full of life-in love with life! Their love for each other was surely a result of answered-prayer!

In Mark 2:24 we find Jesus saying:

"Therefore, I say unto you, what things so ever you desire, when you pray, believe that you receive them, and you shall have them."

True love came a little bit later for Jean. But I'm sure she would tell us that it was well worth the wait. Yet Jean, through the help of a wise friend turned her waiting into a constructive one. She began to expose herself to positive opportunities to meet eligible men. She attended meetings, services, and other spiritual events that gave her a chance to see and be seen.

Understand there are those who would advise that one should just stay home and wait on the Lord to send someone. If that certain someone does not materialize, these advisors would quickly point out that it must not be God's will. Somehow that kind of logic does not set well with me. I agree with that wise woman that was able to help Jean with additional spiritual insight. *"If the Lord wanted you to be a eunuch for Him, He would not have allowed you to have at the same time that deep longing in your breast to love and be loved by a (special person of the opposite sex)."*

Our advice is to suggest a balance in everything. One should not overdo the exposure. Don't feel that you have to run to everything going on with the thought that it's now or never. The Bible teaches that all things be done in moderation. You don't have to run; neither do you have to sit in the shadows expecting perpetual gloom!

Even though I've just finished telling you not to sit home in a closet with the shades drawn, and the lights out expecting to find the man, or woman of your dreams, here is one for the record. A friend told me about his church secretary. She was a single woman who distinguished herself as one of the best. She made herself content with what turned out to be her life's work. Her duties included scheduling church activities; managing church business and sharing the executive load with an elderly pastor. She was a behind the scenes person. According to my friend, this lady was so buried in her heavy load, she rarely had any social life. Mary, now in her retiring years had long since given up any hope of getting married. In the Southland, an elder minister had, about six months before, buried his wife of many years. He remembered that years before while attending a church conference, he had been quickly introduced to the busy secretary of the host congregation. Their meeting was just in passing. I'm sure, that since they were in the same denomination, it is likely that they could have passed each other during conferences, and conventions. Yet, my friend, declares that they must have been nearly like strangers. Well anyway, one day the thought of Mary being his new wife hit him and propelled him into action. He dashed off to where he thought she would be. There she was, still busy and buried. Like a knight on a white charger he came in and rescued her from her church books, and calendars. He swept her off her feet! How he ever found her is amazing. He lost no time like the merchant of the scriptures liquidating all to redeem a pearl of great price. One interesting post script: The church who never thought of Mary in any other way other than the secretary, was shocked to see how quickly she dropped her pad and pencil, and adjusted to being the loving first lady of the elder's castle. Where did she learn all of that? What did she know about loving a man-taking care of a man? How did this church hermit beat out a whole field of potential queen bees, whom I am sure did not hesitate in the buzzing? All this and she never even left the safety of the office. Although I'm sticking to my earlier statements, we realize that there are sometimes exceptions to the rules! Everything needs to be seasoned with prayer and observation. And after finishing that, go back and pray and observe some more.

CHAPTER 3

DATING, LOOKING AT OUR BACKGROUNDS

I HAVE A feeling that there are factors other than the lack of knowhow, that affects the communication between daters. There is a lot of commercial media hype that puts a lot of pressure on couples unwittingly. We are told to use toothpaste that will whiten and brighten our smiles to make us *"kissing sweet"*. To aid us further, there are any number of mouthwashes and sprays on the market. Last but not least, we are reminded to always carry a good supply of breath candy mints. I love those Certs commercials where the people bump into each other and fall in love. We are led to believe that they fall for each other because of their flower fresh breath. Personally I believe it was the bump that done it!

Now there is nothing wrong with the aforementioned items. But the point is that they all are said to be designed to enhance our kissing ability. That can lead us to thinking that a good part of our date has to be kissing! It is my contention that very often when couples should be talking, sharing their personal philosophies, dreams and so on, that precious time is being wasted on improving kissing skills. Certainly, a part of love is physical pleasure, but if love is only physical pleasure, what happens when physical abilities are unable to respond to the assumed level of performance? If Susan catches a bad cold and is unable to transfer her normal germs for a few days—does this mean that it is all over? *"That's stupid,"* you say! I agree, but I'm afraid that as stupid as it sounds there are a lot of people building romances on a shaky foundation like the ability to kiss well.

In our freshman year there was Lance and his girlfriend Irma. Both were rather bright students and both very much in love. There was one noticeable problem with their relationship. Very seldom were they observed talking with each other. Normally you see people in love interacting about issues and answers. Taking the pro and the con. Engaging in discussions about the deep, complicated things, and issues that make individuals unique. We never saw this side of Lance and Irma. Publicly what we saw instead was their great desire for each- others' affection. This they greatly lavished on each other, again exercising reasonable taste. No one ever questioned his or her morals. They always remained within the bounds of acceptable behavior. What most of us thought that their actions were just plain silly! There were those times when we would see one of them say three or four romantic words of some kind. Before the other one would answer back they would have to go through a romantic ritual ending up with a sweet little kiss. If it started with Lance after the kiss it was Irma's time to answer. She would say her few little words and then bang-the kissing again! You would see them all over the campus hugging, smooching-so much in love-to me almost sickening! I can't ever remember seeing this couple engage in serious non-romantic conversation. But I think they did get married and live happily ever after. Listen, kissing is fine, but there is far more use for one's mouth as a communication tool in the dating arena.

Even for those just dating with no serious intentions, it is not out of order to begin learning some basic information. Make it your business to learn something about the other person's background. Family background is vastly important when it comes to character molding and building. I have watched with interest a wife whose parents and grandparents I've known over the years. Her family broke up when she was just a toddler. Even though she was raised by her father and really never knew her mother I can see some of her mother's traits in her. So, bloodlines are sometimes admittedly important. However, I'm not as big on bloodlines as I am on environment. I would not minimize blood ties as it affects certain traits, but that day to day combat training forms the soldier.

The term background covers a large area of life. It includes the social, the religious, the cultural, the educational, and the philosophical aspects of one's life.

I happen to disagree with some of my colleagues who believe that the more diverse the backgrounds; the more exciting the marriage is likely to be. Now if they are talking about diversity of experiences I might find some agreement there. An experience is usually a personal observation or participation in some event, or events. On the other hand, I look at background as more directly resulting from a more deliberate pattern of training, or exposure. We would have of course to include incidental experiences that we have as part of our background also, but their role is not as significant.

More years of experience in counseling has caused me to conclude that the more similar the basic backgrounds, the better the chance for a well-balanced marriage relationship. Now do not misunderstand me. I am not saying that it cannot work with people with diverse backgrounds. What I am saying is that I feel the chance for a happy balance is greater with similar backgrounds. With a similar basic background there is more ground for understanding. The more ground a couple has for understanding the more likely healing can occur when something goes wrong. Again, I am not endorsing extremes.

While in college I knew of a pastor in a mid-western city who let it be known to all of her single parishioners that she wanted them to marry within the congregation. I happened to be going with a girl in this congregation and felt the pressure that loyal members put on me as an outsider. I remember one lady claimed the Lord gave her a dream, telling her that this young lady was to marry Sonny. This was obviously not me! I remember remarking, *"Gee if you know the Lord, and I know the Lord, you would think he'd talk to us!"*

I do praise the Lord that this was not the girl He gave me to marry; I'm Sure, the Lord's hand was at work, but even then, I knew that this pastor's approach was wrong. Time has proven her to be very wrong. Some of these couples forced into wedlock from such a narrow field of choice have ended up with huge problems as a result of the forced matching.

Carmella and Tim are examples of an unbalanced situation. Carmella was born and raised under strict codes of conduct. Family loyalty was primary. She was also exposed to a strong female dominance in the family. Not long after coming to Philadelphia she met Tim, a tall handsome man. Almost before they knew what hit them, they were married. They knew almost nothing of each other's history. Tim never told her that he had been under the care of a psychiatrist for a while. Tim had very little concept of family. He easily jumped from one project to another. His concerns were usually selfish. His family had never been close. He, like Carmella had never known his father. The only male image that Tim had was some older brothers who could care less about the family, each other, or anything else. Tim lavished himself with expensive clothes, furnishings, and gadgets. Money was for having fun! Carmella however, felt that a family should save for important things. She wanted her husband to save with her for a home and the appropriate furniture. While growing up, her family was very poor, but owning a home was very traditional. Her goal was to buy something that her visiting relatives would attribute to a high financial standing. Fancy clothes in a borrowed closet were not the status symbols she counted on.

They never seemed to agree. Carmella worked hard and saved independent of her husband. She literally had to hide her money from the man she was supposed to be closest to. He resented her not sharing her money. Tim spent everything he got his hands on. In fact, his spending habits always out-ran his paying habits. He plunged deeper and deeper into debt. Since his wife was working, after a while, he saw no reason to help out with the family bills. Needless to say, this couple drifted further and further apart. Perhaps if when they were dating they had spent enough time talking about their individual philosophies they would have seen trouble coming.

Understand dating is the beginning of a process. We cannot expect to learn everything in the world about the other person by dating them. However, this author feels that it should give some important insights. These insights should be regarded as serious indicators of the underlying person. It would also seem that the longer people know each other the better their chance at getting to know each other. There are many areas of behavior to be observed. One such area is in the area of finance. know that one of the major problem areas in many marriages is a financial one. Take some note of the spending habits of your date. Does he or she throw money around like water? This could indicate a careless attitude towards finances and spending. Some attitudes are very deeply rooted in us and will not change easily, if at all.

Then there is the other extreme; the person you are dating scrimps and squeezes every little red cent, even when there is no apparent budget crunch. This could indicate a stingy selfish attitude. I was watching a program on TV the other day and they were talking to this husband who was all into the new green movement. So much so that he collected used paper towels from his office bathroom to bring home to reuse because he wanted to recycle them. That's crazy! Who needs to recycle germs? That's going beyond green. Sometimes seeing the spending habits of the female dater are not as easily seen because in our society the male still tends to do the major financing of the date. But still I feel that the fellow through careful observation can get some idea of a girl's attitude about money. If a couple is committed to honesty, I think they will not mind talking about these differences in attitudes, whether it be money, education, religion, sex, or anything else relating to character, personality, and lifestyle. I do think that the conversation about sex attitudes needs to come when a couple is well along in their relationship. There is nothing wrong with gathering information for a possible future. Wait though, until you say, *"I do"*. Do not sexually try to test drive your relationship. that's a bad idea! Again, I must give a word of caution about expecting great changes. Attitudes are built over a period of time. Some with time, commitment, and instruction may change. Many will not change significantly. Over time we know that no one remains exactly the same, but to try to calculate and maneuver those changes would be foolish. Remember how foolish Claude was? He fell so much in love with Belinda he did not even care about major differences. She said at one point that she refused to give up all of her male friends and felt that there was nothing wrong in seeing them from time to time. Claude did not like it but thought that she would change in time! I can still hear those sickening words he uttered, *"Rev, in time I believe she'll come around to my side."* Although I am not into violence, I recall an overwhelming temptation to hit him with my Bible. This was sheer lunacy. In less than a year I listened to him on the other end of the telephone in horror. *"Rev. I heard you talking to me today. I heard you talking to me while I was down in the basement loading up my shotgun. I planned to go upstairs and . . ."* Many times, following that event I have thanked God for helping me to say some right things that stuck and helped to prevent a tragedy.

CHAPTER 4

SHOULD WE DATE, GET ENGAGED OR END IT?

Do not continue to date when you see it leading towards what could be a possible problematic marriage. Thinking that the other person will greatly change for the better? Seldom, if ever does this happen. Sometimes changes do occur but they can be for worst as well as for better! It is better to be satisfied with eyes open that what you have is what you have, before going into a marriage. Deal with the reality that you have rather than to expect drastic improvements later. People just don't change all that much! Open up your eyes and see what you can see right now. Don't fall head over heels in love with someone that you passed overall the warning signs. Trust me they are usually there!

Gwendolyn and Adam should have terminated their relationship from day one. Adam was working his way through Night College when they met. He worked hard driving a taxi during the day trying to salt away enough money to cover his meager living expenses, pay tuition and buy books. One day Gwennie walked into his life and he fell headlong in love. I'm not sure just what he saw in her that sent his heart skipping.

Perhaps it was the fact that she was a professional woman. She was fairly attractive physically, but of greater attraction perhaps was her poise and obvious cultural background. Her family was pretty wealthy and she was used to living very comfortably.

In spite of the love he had for her something deep in his mind was bothering Adam about their relationship. He could not quite put his finger on it. So, he sought counseling. Someone once suggested that if your first mind raises a caution flag you should probably follow that first mind even though the second mind wants to over-rule that caution.

After he related the story to me, I could see what that deep seated caution was about. Adam could also see it, but he was afraid to admit it on a conscious level. He wanted to be courageous and not back out on her even though down inside he knew it was going wrong.

After hearing the story, I discovered that Gwennie was a very selfish lady. She was in her early thirties, never married and used to living in a high style. Indeed, she was high maintenance. When they dated she wanted him to take her to the best places and spend money that he really did not have to spend. She insisted that he fit into her world. His world as a struggling student was not an option. Even though he would have a promising career down the road. Adam had to work more overtime just to try to keep up. Yet this did not seem to make much of a difference to her.

This went on because Adam shut his eyes to the truth. Perhaps one of the understandable things that drew him to her was that she had led him into a relationship with the Lord. How can you not love the person who brings you to Christ? Later, this relationship with the Lord proved to be the most positive thing to come out of this story. In addition to a spiritual experience he wanted a family; a wife, children, but most of all someone to rest his heart safely with. He dreamed of what could be, while closing his eyes to what was. Soon they were engaged and there was in his mind no turning back. Perhaps the reader can see why I believe dating to be so crucial. **It takes no great talent to fall in love**. It is not any more difficult to fall in love with the wrong person. People do it all the time!

I recall this being the only time as a counselor becoming so emotionally involved with a client that I found tears walling up inside. I had to actually turn my head as the tears began to slip hotly down my cheeks. The moment that pushed it over my emotional edge was when Adam opened his work uniform jacket to expose an almost missing lining, worn out by continued usage. Then he showed me his shoe soles. They were punched clear through with cardboard inserts placed inside to keep his feet off the ground. Adam was no bum. Actually, he was a very proud man working very hard to make it to the top. He sacrificed to buy an engagement ring far beyond his means. Honestly it would have been far beyond my means. It was what Gwendolyn wanted. Add to that list the wedding, the honeymoon abroad, an expensive apartment with a view, a new car, and on and on. Her demands really put the *"H. I."* in high maintenance.

Was Adam crazy to go for all of this? No Adam was just in love. In love with a dream. What was it Gwendolyn wanted? After this marriage broke up (far less than a year) my conclusion was that Gwen wanted the one thing that she didn't have? In her profession it just looked real- good to be a *"Mrs. Adam".*

During the dating period or any time prior to the actual marriage, a relationship should *be open to termination*. If you see it won't work forget about the embarrassment of breaking up. It may be a collision on the way. I knew a couple that had one last chance, the night before the wedding to terminate their nuptial plans. The bride-to-be snapped-out for no apparent reason. She actually stormed out of their wedding practice. Something in her subconscious mind happened that was never sufficiently explained. But the invitations were out, the presents purchased and all was ready. Trust me, termination would have saved them many years of heartache. In those days I was kind of new in pasturing. Looking back, I wish that I could have suggested for them to back up for a minute and take a second look. Inexperience wanted to save them from embarrassment so we foolishly went on with it. What benefit is there to trying to make the unworkable workable? Before you plunge headlong into a nightmare, *terminate the relationship*. After you've ignored all of the warning signs and gone ahead with the permanence of marriage you have entered into a whole new set of circumstances.

MORE ABOUT MOVING INTO MARRIAGE

When I first began as a marriage counselor I discovered Walter Trobish's triangular marriage platform based on Genesis 2:24:

> *"Therefore, shall a man leave his father and his mother and shall cleave unto his wife: And they shall be one flesh."*

Trobish went on to further define this passage as the leaving being the element of the law, the cleaving the element of love, and one flesh as sex. Later I adopted Tim LaHaye's term for sex as being the *"Marriage act"*. This three-fold breakdown does seem to be very consistent with scripture. I've since made it the basis for my teaching on the subject of marriage. Often when problems occur in the marriage, they develop in one of these three areas. Then if not checked and corrected they spread to the remaining two areas. More will be said about this Triangular Plan in later chapters. For now, our purpose for introduction is to show that it can affect daters as well as marriage partners.

COMMUNICATION TIES IT TOGETHER

Picture three large pearls strung through with a thin silver chain to make a valuable necklace. We would refer to it hanging in a jewelry display as a pearl necklace. Think of the necklace as representing a marriage. The three pearls represent the three elements, Leaving, Cleaving and One flesh, each very valuable. Yet you don't have a necklace until they are strung together. I've chosen silver because it is a precious metal. The precious string running through, binding these three elements together is verbal communication. That is how important good communication is for dating couples and marriage partners alike.

It is amazing that many daters spend so very little time when it comes to real verbal communication. Communication is an important key when it comes to great relationships. In school, we were taught that in order to have successful communication going, three main things were involved:

1. *You have to have a message*
2. *You have to have a sender*
3. *You have to have a receiver*

These three elements must work together almost in a circular fashion. First the sender issues a message to the receiver who in turn issues a response back to the original sender who is now the receiver. This is ideally how it is supposed to work. Even with these three constants operating there is no guarantee at this point that the complete message has gone from sender to receiver with understanding. According to the communication formula much depends on what does not get in the way. A message can be blocked, interrupted, deflected, refracted, fractured, and even rejected! Add to this the possibility that a message can also just plainly be misunderstood. Perhaps we can settle on a simple definition of the kind of vital verbal communication we are promoting: It is the *conveying of an honest thought by way of talking and honest listening.* The sender of the message must first of all be committed to sharing an honest thought without submerging it in 'gobbaly goop'. This is when one sugar coats it so heavily that the true content is masked. Who really knows what was said? The sender must also not strive for a raw shock appeal that is offensive, rude and in bad taste. I heard about a survey that was taken many years ago when Howard Stern was on a New York radio station. It said that most of his listeners listened to him not because they liked what he was saying, but in disbelief of what he was going to say next. Don't follow his example. Say what you mean, without it being mean and offensive when saying it! Consider the merits of these three statements concerning a fellow whose date is offended by his heavy use of garlic:

1. *"Sam whenever I'm with you I'm so impressed with your love for imported garlic. Eating with you and your Gourmet garlic choices is certainly, a challenge I'm looking forward to dubiously!"*
2. *"Sam your breath stinks! That nasty garlic you always eat could drop a wild hog at thirty feet."*
3. *"Sam whenever I'm with you and you've eaten garlic, it turns me off. Would you please make a special effort before our dates, to forgo eating it? Thank you!"*

The first statement drips with sugar, but is totally dishonest in coming to grips with what seems to be a problem. In this first statement, the speaker seems to indicate that she is attracted to Sam's garlic. But this is seen to be untrue by the last word, *"dubiously,"* used in the statement. A person using this kind of almost flattering method may feel that they are sparing the other person's feelings, but in reality, is setting a pattern of not telling the truth that may continue and even deepen its' roots in the relationship. I am sure that an unchecked pattern of not telling the truth, begun in the dating period and allowed to continue in the marriage will hurt that marriage. When does honesty begin? It is unlikely that a practice such as lying will ever terminate itself without genuine repentance and reform. Remember that only the power of God applied to personal resolve can bring about a steadfast commitment. Lying is a sin and it will not ultimately help. The second statement made to Sam may be the truth but the rawness of the delivery can only bring about hurt and offense. Is the speaker really hoping that after hearing such raw information, that Sam might alter his behavior? The message being shared must have a purpose or goal. If a message is only given to insult the listener, then the purpose is very shallow. Sometimes in dating, an ugly pattern can be set into motion by saying something careless. After it is said and the regrets come, it is a little late to try and reel it back in. Think before you speak. Try to say it in the very best manner that conveys the message clearly with sensitivity. Have you ever observed a married couple who treat each other with little or no respect? Insults are traded as a matter of course in their conversation. I remember Pam and Donavan a couple we used to hang out with in our early years. Most of the time we were with them they found funny things that were not too funny to say about each other. Actually, they were criticizing and blaming each other on the sleigh. They lacked the courage and honesty to just sit down and say, *"Listen I just don't like it when you do thus- and so"*. *"If you could, make, an effort to do better at this it would really please me"*. Rather than work it out in the trenches they would sneak-a-tell it in a public joke.

A married couple like this has come to accept these insults as normal behavior. However, this behavior is in violation of the principles of respect and honor found in 1Peter 3:1-13. Along with that Jesus also teaches another principle that we must love our neighbor as our self. If we follow His pattern two things become quickly apparent: *We must develop a healthy respect for our personal self, and that same kind of respect for our neighbor.* Truly loving and respecting someone else must spring out of a healthy acceptance of one's self.

Because I love you, when you engage in a behavior that is offensive to me, for relationship sake, I should tell you honestly in the kindest way I can so that seeds of bitterness do not form and grow. The Bible also warns us against trying to cover up by hiding oughts' (*that is an old word for disputes, grievances, insults, and personal disturbance, etc.)* that have dug deeply into us. We have an obligation to straighten out these *'little foxes'* that end up sapping life out of the vine. Gardeners know that sometimes on fruit trees little branches appear on the bottoms of the trees. These are sometimes referred to as *"suckers"*. So, these gardeners will carefully remove them because they sap the life out of the rest of the tree. Our third statement to Sam is forthright and frank. It is factual but done kindly. It offers the important element of hope. You get the feeling that if Sam makes an honest effort to avoid the garlic before their date, that everything will be fine. There is no implication that the conversation needs to go any further than his concession.

When we communicate we convey honest thought by way of forthright conversation in the hope that the person on the receiving end will make every attempt to understand without coloring, adding to, or taking away from the text, or context of that message.

A dishonest listener does not help the process at all. I'm sure we all know persons who hear what they want to hear. But in the end does it serve the ending of the matter? When I'm in a discussion with someone and I find out that the other person wants to hear it only the way they want to hear I turn off. I want to hear what you have to say. I must believe that what you are saying is coming from your heart. I need to examine what you are saying in the light you are sharing it. When then it is my turn to share I want you to hear from my heart. If a compromise is needed it should be stimulated by our honest efforts to communicate the true feelings we have. We may not agree on every point in life but it is certainly good to hear each other out, and make an attempt at finding middle ground. Sometimes the compromise is stronger than either of the personal positions.

CHAPTER 5

THE LEAVING FACTOR

DATING, ALTHOUGH OFTEN thought of as being something innocent can lead to an eventual marriage. So, we need to think more seriously about where dating might go as an end result. Again, we are not saying that you will marry everyone you date. That would be a ridiculous statement. However, it is pretty likely you will date the one you marry. So we need to examine some foundational truths that will help in the selection process. Understanding some of the things you observe about those you are dating may very well save some eventual heartbreak. On the other hand, it may help to prevent losing out on a potentially great relationship that during the early dating period just did not seem to click.

So, if you are **just dating** at this point and feel that you can skip this section because where you are, is not that serious, **please don't skip here**. There is important information that you may need to know later on in your life.

A basic foundation for marriage is found the first time in Genesis 2:24 *"a man is to leave his father and his mother, cleave to his wife, and the two shall become one flesh".* I call this God's triangular plan. It provides the full support system for any marriage. There are three main elements in God's system. This seems so simple, almost too simple for some. Let me remind you that the triangle is the strongest of the geometric shapes. A load placed upon the pinnacle of a triangle of substantial materials will bear that weight as long as the points hold together. This is due to the weight being distributed evenly along the whole system. Actually, it helps itself sustain itself. The architecture of Buckminster Fuller often utilized the strength of the triangle. In fact, Fuller created a ball-like dome made from combined triangles. From this we could draw an interesting parallel: If the triangle represents the family the dome could represent the larger community. The obvious conclusion to our parallel illustration is that a strong society is made up of strong families.

Scriptural/spiritually each of these three elements is substantial; together they are powerful. However just as a physical triangle becomes defeated when any of the elements are removed the same becomes true in the business of marriage. Without each of these elements working together in tandem, distributing the weight along the entire foundation of the marriage, the marital union will grow weaker and weaker until a second element is adversely affected. If at this point the condition is not corrected look for either a total collapse of the union, or a very ineffective marriage. A marriage that remains by mutual agreement based on, *"For the sake of the children",* or *"It would not look good in the public right now",* as reasons, *or "Think what this would do to our parents after having invested so much in our happiness,"* etc. The excuses go on and on but lead to nothing positive. Staying married has little to do with other people and what they think. Yes it does affect the children but you need to stay for you. After all, one day you promised through sickness and health and all that other stuff that you would remain.

Our society is not in the greatest shape today because of so many weak families. Each family unit does have an effect on the whole of society. If you imagine that each marriage is like a drop in the bucket just remember that continual drops will eventually over flow the bucket.

LEAVING IS A REAL FACTOR

The very first leg of our Genesis triangle is called leaving. The leaving element is the lawful public separation from one's former parent/child family structure to a new permanent commitment of fidelity, love and equal partnership between one man and one woman. This is the only scriptural and even sensible societal basis for marriage to exist. These are the only possibilities for nature to be satisfied and for offspring to be born. There may be those who feel that by including *offspring being born* within this text, provides a loophole to develop an argument for same-sex marriages. They would say what about a heterosexual union that produces no children? Would not this also cancel out any marriage without children? My friend there is your answer. With a heterosexual couple there always lies the genetic possibility of producing an offspring. The homosexual alliance, on the other hand, could never naturally produce children. Genetically it is not possible. Even if we stretched toward a science-fiction scenario where somehow an egg could be carried and delivered by a male, he certainly could never have originally produced that egg. And of course, if it were two women trying to reproduce, the egg would have to be stimulated by male sperm, which neither of them could do. Wow, God is so smart! So again, the leaving element is the lawful public separation from one's former parent/child family structure to a new permanent commitment of fidelity, love and equal partnership between one man and one woman.

LEAVING HOME

The previous attachments and dependencies in the parent/child relationship should be dissolved and restructured within the new relationship. One's Dad will always be one's Dad but the measure of direct influence upon daily decisions is drastically altered by time and experience. In our family we would not expect our married children to call us up about every decision they had to make. In those few areas that they did consult with us they would only be asking for focus and clarity. Even then we should not expect them to just accept every direction we see as being the answer. If they ask for advice, we realize that the final decision is up to them. While we were raising them we were teaching format, direction, and focus. When they go out on their own it is likely that their backgrounds will kick in. So, it is unlikely in a family where strong, responsible parenting is going on that those children will go very far from those principles that they learned. Does that now 'GROWN-UP' need to go back constantly to their, initial source to check for answers? I'm sure your answer to that question is *"No"*. It is probably like college for most of us. The college provided for us more than mere subject matter. It presented to us a way of thinking. It gave to us a method of developing thought, seeking out information through research, and then developing a method of presentation. Can you imagine every time we had to develop an argument, a presentation, or a project, flying back to the campus to find Dr. Head to help us? No! It doesn't work that way! The college we went to and learned from, is now in us!

LEAVING FRIENDS

In the realm of leaving home there's another group to be considered. Friends often pose a real threat to the comfort level of the new couple. Sometimes one's friends have been lifelong companions who have shared secrets, fears, and other intimacies. Suddenly one valued friend has invited a new person into their life and placed this new person in a place that is now above where the original friendship was. This is a difficult place for both persons. The new spouse wants to continue to love the former friend but often feels drawn between those old love relationships and their new spouse. The old friend may actually feel jealous of the spousal relationship.

Wanda and Artia had been lifelong friends since kindergarten. They rode the school bus together until they finished high school. There wasn't anything that they did not share. Even during their four years of college they were separated by only a few blocks. Following graduation Wanda met Frank and fell madly in love with him. This was not a problem at first because they became a trio often going places together. After a while Artia noticed Wanda and Frank planning things without her. Then a final straw came when she just happened to hear about Wanda's engagement from another friend. She felt hurt and left out. Even though she was asked to be Wanda's Maid of Honor she knew that things would never be the same.

Never the same but precious is possible. When God separates the past with the leaving clause it is designed to forge a brand-new unit into existence. All of the former supporting units, such as parents, friends, and church members, etc. should now formulate new surrounding support units that help to protect the sanctity of the marriage. Chelsea, another friend of Wanda and Frank, helped Artia to see that they could be of valuable help to the new couple from the outside in. They did not have to know the couple's day-to-day business, but there were some obvious things that friends could do to help them. One was that Frank needed a better job. Chelsea knew a friend that knew a friend that worked in an office that needed a qualified manager with Frank's skills. The word was passed and Frank got the job. Then Wanda got pregnant sooner than they planned. Artia was able to help with some of the babysitting between the couple's working shifts. Still friends but now a different supportive relationship. Artia could have just sat and stewed over the changes in their relationship but when her eyes were opened she saw needs that she could relate to. Because they loved each other she wanted to meet these needs. True friendship is willing to have flexibility built-in. Growth demands flexibility.

LEAVING OLD NOTIONS

Leaving home also involves the dissolving of preconceived negative notions. These negative notions may cause a bias in the new nest building process. We've all heard those supposed to be funny stories and jokes about the hardship of marriage. Most of them paint pictures that do not applaud marriage. Negative notions can provide a base for dim expectations. Dimmed expectations lack little hope of anything better than what was expected in the first place. Example: Johnnie Mae grew up hearing from her mother that, *"All men were dogs". "All they want to do is give you babies to keep you tied down so you can't check on them and their other women."* It didn't help any that her own father made this description larger than life. When Johnnie Mae grew up and got married to Willie, who actually was a good man, she only saw what her negative training had presented, taught and engraved. She held onto the stereotypes and magnified any shortcomings and simple human failings. She did this so much that she could not even see the gem she had. Sad to say, their marriage failed because she couldn't let go of the negative images in someone else's story that she embraced. The principle here is found in Philippians 4:8 which deals with what we place in our minds, and what we allow to remain there. *"Whatsoever things are true, whatsoever things are honest, whatsoever things are just, whatsoever things are pure, whatsoever things are lovely, whatsoever things are of good report…think on these things."*

There's a somewhat new negative notion that has come on the scene practiced by some of the rich and famous. May it die there and never have a chance to reach the less than rich. I'm talking about what is now called a 'Prenuptial agreement'. When one has money and marries someone without money or when two people with separate monies get married they may seek to draw up a prenuptial agreement. In this author's opinion this is pre-cursing the marriage before it can get started. It actually says, *"When this marriage fails your money will stay with you and mine will stay with me".*

I respect a lot financial counselor Suze Orman in her practical approach to financial responsibility. However, I sharply disagree with her views concerning the prenuptial agreement. I suppose it makes all the sense in the world when you come from a practical secular point of view. Again Ms. Orman would warn that should divorce become a factor the female especially must be prepared financially to go on with her life. This again, according to the world only makes good sense. However, after one studies the Bible, God's concept of marriage is vastly different from world logic. It is not incidental that we find words like trust, hope, faith, etc. so often repeated in the Bible as they relate to human behavior. The Biblical principle deals with what we place in our minds, and what we allow to remain there. Scripture teaches us to be people of hope. *"... Whatsoever things are true, honest, just, pure, lovely, and of a good report ... think on these things.* (Phil.4: 8) these are the things that we are to allow in our minds. Our hope springs forth from what is on the inside. Without hope coupled with faith and trust, one can't really begin a solid marriage. The prenuptial document may be on the surface built on a premise of, *"if it fails"*, but the underlying reality is, *"when it fails"*! If a person who is intending to be married does not feel comfortable exposing their spouse to-be to all of their' money, then they should not get married until they do, or until they find that someone in whom they can trust. After all it is called marriage! Financial stress can be found in the top three causes for marital breakdown. If one announces up front that there is a lack of trust, then what can be expected to result later on? Power from the principle comes when we, "Speak it, write it, and perform it"! So many times, I heard my, grandfather, the late Elder Daniel Barnes say, *"Words are like people. They run up ahead of you and wait for you to catch up with them."* In one way it's like saying that our words become our predictors and our guides. We give birth to them and then follow them obediently hand in hand, destined to follow them on their prescribed path.

Scripture again teaches us to be a people of hope. The things that are true, honest, just, pure, lovely and of good report: these are the things that we are to allow into our minds. Our hope springs forth from what is on the inside. Hope based on nothing is at its best only presumption.

LEAVING WHAT ARE MY NEEDS?

When a person contemplates marriage even before they begin to actively look for a mate, some self-evaluation should go on. (2 Cor.11: 28) Says *"let a man examine himself,"* which refers to communion, but the stronger text related to our subject is actually found in Luke chapter 14: 28-30, *"for which of you intending to build a tower does not sit down first and count the cost . . .?* Actually, let's call it, NEEDS ASSESSMENT. Investigate the needs and desires that you feel in need of. Internally discuss and evaluate this list; making sure that the items are constant and non-negotiable. They need to be more stable than just a wish list. My brother used to ask his wife when she was on her way to the mall whether she was actually going shopping or window wishing? The wish list is good, but also know those items on your needs list that are negotiable and can be traded off. We all probably include things that we desire but are really not necessary to insure our future happiness and wellbeing.

When one has found that special one to leave father and mother for, it should be with an informed hope. Yet hope based on nothing is at its best only a presumption. One should investigate their own needs and desires and evaluate the ability of that special person to meet those needs and desires.

I heard a very good friend of our family talk about how she agreed to marry another longtime friend of our family. They had both lost their first spouse by death. Cathy said that she had been working on a project in the same town that Wesley lived in. He heard about her project and decided to be her prayer partner to help get it accomplished on time. Every morning he would call her before he left for work to have a word of prayer. Everyday Cathy's work went well and all of the daily objectives were more than met. In the evenings Wes would call to check on her progress. They laughed and talked and visited by phone for what seemed like hours when in fact these calls were not very long at all. Occasionally they saw each other when Cathy needed some additional help on her project. Their meetings were never in anyway romantic. Just business between two emerging friends! One evening just as Cathy was ending her project in that town Wes called. Instead of his normal inquiry about the day's success he asked her to marry him. Cathy was in total shock. She had never thought of him in this way. She found herself politely declining his offer. Perhaps it was their age difference since she was several years his senior. Maybe she had thought that her husband to-be would come from her own community or be located in her local church-group. Who knows just why she felt initially that the offer was just not an answer to her prayers? It was 3AM that morning after not being able to sleep, she decided to reevaluate her position. She thought of her list of needs and desires. *"Guess what"*, she explains, *"This man met nearly every one of these items. If he did not come in on the top of the list in a mere few items, he was so close to the top that the difference wasn't even worth noting"*. Her heart leaped! Wes was the man!

Her man! She said, *"I had to tell him so. It was a little after 3AM in the morning. I had to hurry so that some other women wouldn't suddenly awaken and discover this fine man and beat me out"*! They have as a postscript, continued to live happily ever after.

Long before you become engaged to get married and prepare to leave home, and all that goes on with that, develop a personal list of needs and desires. Ideally do it in advance of the romantic arrival of Mr. Right or Miss Right. If you wait until then the usual thing is more like designing a project that includes the current landscape. Usually in such a project you plan around what is already there. But if you begin dreaming and planning before you have the real estate, you are free to pull out of yourself the genuine desires that are not based on what the land looks like. If you are single and looking, why not give, prayerful consideration to these needs and desires. In fact, why not try brainstorming for ideas?

Take a sheet of paper and write down every possible item you can think of, or ask for, relating to the kind of person you are looking for. It is a private list that no one else will see so don't edit or sensor this list. Just put the ideas down as they come. After you have exhausted your mind developing your **'Wish list'**; begin separating this still unedited list into two columns on a second piece of paper. On the left side of the sheet recopy all of the things that can be recognized as bona fide **Needs**, such as: *honest, loving, sharing, a Christian, loves home and family, etc. Other* things in your list might be *someone who is a financial provider, or one who is an encourager, or a sound spiritual leader.* These are the types of things that would be on the needs side of your list:

Now in the column on the right- side list those items that are your **Wants or Desires**: *handsome, tall, drives a nice car, owns a house, is a teacher, goes to my church, must be shorter than I am. Others might add that the person must fit into a certain weight or body shape, and must be between the age of this or that.* The items in this list may be our strong desires but as you can see are really negotiable. Again, don't edit these items yet.

There may be some items that you are not sure where they fit. Either place them into the one that suits the item best, or list them on the reverse side for now.

Now is the time to pray:

> *"Lord now that I have emptied myself, help me to see clearly what should be. Give me the maturity and willingness to see things in their proper perspective. Help me to eliminate that which in its' finality will prove useless".*
> *Amen*

If you are married and experiencing some second thoughts about you and your spouse's comfort level perhaps developing a list of needs might prove helpful. What is it that you really need? Start your unedited list in the same way that singles have been instructed. Let the items flow freely. Again put your ideas of what you alone need just as they come. When you have exhausted your mind and nothing else comes, stop. Now begin separating the still unedited list into two columns on a second piece of paper. On the left side of the sheet recopy all of the things that can be recognized as bona fide needs. On the right- side column place the things that are important to you but really are more wants than needs. Again, don't edit just separate. Those things that you can't decide whether they are needs or wants, just place them on the reverse side of the paper for now. This now is your time to pray that same prayer:

> *"Lord now that I have emptied myself, help me to see clearly what should be. Give me the maturity and willingness to see things in their proper perspective. Help me to eliminate that which in its' finality will prove useless".*
> *Amen*

This is where your task differs from the singles' assignment. You will ask your spouse to develop the same kind of Needs List and to follow the same brainstorming process including the same prayer. The whole point of preparing these lists is to share the lists with each other. This time I want you to pray that same prayer again but together before you begin sharing item #1 from the Needs list of party A. It does not matter particularly who goes first since our plan is to discuss every item on both lists. Discuss honestly whether that need is being met. If it is being met then appreciation should be expressed to that spouse. If not being met then it is an opportunity for a willing spouse to be made aware. So often spouses are unaware of just what the real needs of their mates are. By simply talking about them one at a time a new understanding may be in your future. After the first party's first item has been fairly expressed and discussed then begin disclosure and discussion about the first item on the second spouse's list. Just keep alternating until all the items on both lists are addressed. Try to find agreement in as many areas as you can. Continue to ask God to help you in your understanding and desire to meet, as best you can, your spouse's needs.

Needs are crucial yet desires *are* important too. Don't just eliminate something because it is (only) a desire and somebody told you to only grab the essentials and overlook the silly little nonsensical, nonessential desires. I believe recognizing those personal desires that really are important to us is what helps us to really like some people that we already love. It's kind of like that old story about Henry Ford's remarks on the production of his 'model T'. *"The public can have any color car they want as long as it's black."* Needs for transportation do not take away altogether a desire to express oneself in red, or blue, or even black! If the Ford Company had maintained the sentiments of that statement by old Henry, and produced only black cars, the competition would have driven them from business long ago. Personally, I need to put on clothes. The ones that I choose to put on tell you something about me. Most of the time I happen to feel pretty good in my clothes. I need them but I also appreciate them for many reasons. Looking to find someone who only meets your needs while forgetting about your desires is as bad as having to drive around in a nondescript car that provides only transportation.

Again, the first part of the marriage triangular plan is the leaving factor. Part of the leaving decision is to Leave all others, forsaking the past. This is crucial in order to build the future together. This must be done through an honest self-evaluation of one's readiness. The ability to make an actual list of expectations and decide which are non-negotiable needs, separated from what are preferable desires, calls for a level of maturity. As previously stated these desires are somewhat negotiable.

LEAVING HOME IS NOT MOVING IN

Recently I counseled with a couple who loved each other enough to give birth to several children. However, their real struggles these days are if they can find enough areas that they like about each other so they can get married. Living together without an official commitment has produced a whole host of other problems. We'll deal at this time with the lack of fulfilled desires.

Donna always wanted to marry a champion who would take her away from the ghetto. She wanted someone who would help build her low self esteem, and would allow her to finish her college education. She ultimately wanted to launch a business career. It was hard for her to like Ronald these days. He to her represented the negative of all the above. He never married her even though she gave him seven, or eight years of her life. He had paraded them from one side of the ghetto to the other. He seemed to be out of work more than in it. Building her self-esteem was like a big joke. He found every reason to criticize and ridicule her. Donna was not perfect in Ronald's eyes either. He wanted a wife that was attractive and neat. He said he wanted someone that would work with his ideas and dreams. Donna had allowed herself to get too fat and comfortable. Their house looked like *"who struck Jerusalem!"* He could never do anything right. *"The only idea she had of working with him,"* he said, *"was to stand in the door with her hand out asking for money."* Though there wasn't much to like on either side, history showed that they couldn't stay away from each other. They would break up to make up! Neither of them had a very realistic view of marriage. They moved in together thinking that their dreams and fantasies would be actualized through each other. This was not a good move. They decided to live together like man and wife but without much of a sense of what being married was about.

Somebody just ought to tell folks the truth about this growing-phenomena among many of today's young couples. They make it sound so innocent when they term it *'Living- together'! "Shacking up, living common law"*, are older terms from a different time period! They sound very harsh in today's more politically correct generation. Somebody needs to say to them that the name- change amounts to nothing. The decision to move in and set up a type of Pseudo-marriage, that's kind of a marriage, but that's not really a marriage, is just like drinking poison that has been taken out of its original marked bottle and placed in a substitute bottle that is unmarked. It has the same potential for killing you, no matter what it says on the package. The even older term that nobody likes calls it, **"Living in sin"**!

LEAVING NEEDS TO BE LEGAL

Donna and Ronald's number one problem grows out of their violation of God's number one principle. They were trying to have the benefits of marriage without being married and it just won't work! It may seem exciting, or adventurous at first, but will likely prove poisonous to the relationship. The first step in the 'Triangular Plan', calls for the public leaving of both individuals from their former homes. *A marriage begins with a legal obligation.* It seems almost too simple when it appears in Genesis 2:24: *"A man shall (must) leave his father and mother…"* This statement begins simple enough but don't let those eight words get past you. This was not intended to be a suggestion that these people leave their former ties. It is a declaration of how it must be when they leave! The reference to a man leaving means mankind must leave the former nest, both male and female alike. In every culture there is an understanding that the leaving is a formal one, and that that leaving event is tied in legally. Whether found in an old African-American custom of the couple, *"Jumpin' Da' Broom"* together, or the Hawaiian custom of placing a lei made up of flowers around the necks of the newlyweds, or in the Ghanaian practice of Knocking on the door, there is a formal marriage ceremony. Do the research, even though there are many different ceremonies and traditions, still there is a legal way that; distinguishes the married state from the single state. No matter the custom it still is understood to be a legal launching of a man and wife in a bona fide marriage.

Some years ago, I attended a wonderful ceremony that seemed to be lifted out of the pages of an African fantasy. The whole procession unfolded to the rhythmic voices of African drums that replaced the traditional wedding music of our culture. The grandmother of the groom opened with a wonderful prayer that set the tone, followed by the couple's proud parents dressed in custom clothes befitting the occasion. We watched as they promenaded their way down to the front of the church followed by the entire wedding party; each with their own personal dance steps timed to the cadence of the singing drums. The mothers lit single candles representing their two families before taking their respective seats. The groom abandoned the usual practice of entering from the front with the minister to await his bride. He too danced his dance accompanied by the drums and occasional high -pitched yelps and gurgle sounds. Momentary silence greeted the bride and her father. Then almost mysteriously we heard her prerecorded voice, half chanting—half singing, her love story, frequently reciting and linking the name of her lover with her own as she pranced down the aisle with her proud father.

What an event! This was a treat to behold. Never have I seen it done any better. I appreciated so much their courage to be themselves. With all the gala there was still a legal public declaration of their vows along with communion. In fact, they went one step further. They engaged in the sacrament of 'foot-washing'.

Not stated but observed in those eight words in Genesis 2: 24: *"A man shall (must) leave his father and mother . . ."* is a deep spiritual/emotional/ psychological factor. Without this initial action being in place, a serious wounding of one's inner self occurs. The woman who may fall for the early lines like, *"It doesn't matter-it's only a piece of paper"* . . . or *"Our love is strong enough to hold us together, "* etc. will certainly feel betrayed after a while. She will eventually ask, *"Why am I not good enough to be officially his wife"? Why, is he ashamed of me"?* The woman who is led into living in sin often arrives there because she feels she will lose him if she doesn't hold on to him in this way. In the end she will hardly feel that it was worth it, especially after a breakup. She will likely feel pitiful, helpless, and the self-esteem she was trying to have built will plummet to a new level of low.

The man will also become affected by the living in sin arrangement. Because of her mental/emotional state of being, he will become frustrated, irritated, and helpless. He will feel that all the blame is being placed on him. In the beginning he will try to erase her doubts and fears. But time causes a growing state of unhappiness. This growing state cannot be erased because they are attempting to do something that was never intended to be. When the principles of God are ignored the consequences are severe. It just cannot be fixed up to be anything other than what it is! It is like taking painkiller to hide the effects of a broken foot. If the foot is not set and attended to when the medicine wears off, the pain will still be there. If the problem is not solved the unresolved concerns may actually be compounded because the foot is still broken.

Not too long ago I worked with a couple who was living in the same house. They loved each other and were actually planning to get married within that year. Both claimed to be Christians, and actually went to church faithfully. I sensed a great heaviness in their relationship and began to probe in order to help them. I did not know about their living arrangement at that time. After discovering their situation, I asked each of them why. It was so interesting to listen to each of them share. It would seem that neither of them felt any great comfort in their living together. In fact, as they talked on about how they arrived at this arrangement each of them thought that it was what the other one wanted. The session ended with them falling into each other's arms; each determined to return to living alone until they got married. You could feel the tension in the room go as the peace of God swept over two of His people who vowed to do right. It reminds me of the song that I used to hear on the radio as a little boy. Reverend Bob Frazier, a blind evangelist sang:

I know the Lord will make a way for me,
I know the Lord will make a way for me.
If I live a holy life, shun the wrong and do the right,
I know the Lord will make a way for me!

So, it is with the first leg of our marital triangular system. Leaving publicly is part of God's plan. It satisfies the law of the land; it satisfies God and mysteriously satisfies something in us.

CHAPTER 6

MORE ABOUT LEAVING

ERICA CHOSE TO get married secretly to a man her family did not know, or never even knew existed. For over a year they managed to live as man and wife but chose to tell no one. All kinds of elaborate schemes were devised to guard their secret. It may sound strange but sometimes the results of secret marriages are the same as the folks who are shacking up. I really think that this couple's reasons for the elaborate deception were pretty similar. They wanted to quietly see if it would work. It didn't! It was like a self-fulfilling prophecy. If escape clauses are built into the leaving leg of the triangle whether by secret trial marriage, or a living in sin arrangement, it will likely affect the remaining two legs of the triangle. Remember I found real difficulty with the prenuptial agreement for pretty much the same reasons. There seems to be a genuine need for a couple to be joined in a public way. Part of the genuine joy of being married is to openly enjoy each other. There is no shame attached. There is no hiding of the facts. Legally we have been given the right to declare our love openly. The system for legally leaving, places us in a legally authorized position. It is a must position. Publicly we have declared our willingness to be dependent upon each other. There is no easier way to do it. In the beginning Adam and Eve were thrust together, sink or swim, climb or fall. Interestingly enough even though they did a wrong thing, disregarding God's commandment not to eat the fruit of a certain tree, they both decided to fall together. It is called marriage!

Before moving on to the next chapter where we will explore the second area called cleaving, there are a few more things that we need to examine here. Leaving connotes a separation. Separation here actually means that a new structural relationship begins. Formerly in the single person/ parent relationship the parental input in some situations was wisely quite strong. Many of us while single felt to involve our parents in our major decisions. This should now change in this new call for separation. The child/parental love factor will not—should not change, however, the former emotional attachments and dependencies will realign in a new healthy marriage relationship. Whereas before the marriage, in the child/parent relationship, decisions probably came through reliable dialogue and understanding. The same process is now expected to be in place but now it is between husband and wife. They must become wholly dependent on each other. This was God's intention from the beginning. Again, it is called marriage! Actually, good parenting provides instructions and examples for sound decision-making. I can expect that in life my children are going to make some decisions completely on their own, just the way that their parents would. The reason for that simply follows that all of their lives we have been teaching and reinforcing a process.

When our children were coming up we taught them not to respond to bells, whistles, or cute little tunes played by the 'Ice Cream Man' when he visited the neighborhood. I knew that the theory of *Conditioned Response'* came from a Russian scientist named Pavlov. I was determined not to have my children performing like the scientist's dog when it heard a bell. Well our philosophy worked pretty well we thought until one early summer afternoon. I was working in the little garden in front of our porch pulling weeds or something. When down the street I heard the Jack and Jill Man playing his summoning theme. Almost without hesitation I heard from inside the house the rumble of racing feet, a crash through the screen door, and a sprint across the porch. I stood erect, wiping my brow in disbelief. I hardly saw the speeding image of a child disappearing behind the hedges. *"Who was that,"* I mused? *"It could not have been a Stevens running down the street in response to the Pavlovian call. No way!"* Yet I knew in my mind that it was our youngest child, not known for his conformity to family tradition or policy. Where had we gone wrong? Did my message fall on deaf ears—was there really a concrete helmet preventing penetration up there? While I pondered these things in my heart the young progeny returned empty-handed grumbling. *"Heh, that guy must be crazy asking those prices for that stuff—he must be crazy. I'm not throwing my money away!"* *"Thank you Lord he is a Stevens after all,"* I smiled. Perhaps at the time he was not honing in on the *"Thou shall not . . ."* but the process of economy kicked in. The scriptural principle is to: *"Train up a child in the way he should go . . ."* this principle has a dual meaning:

1. Train children according to the standards and statuettes of the law.
2. Train the child recognizing the individuality of that child and the particular needs and characteristics associated with that child.

So, we can associate the above for anxious parents who struggle to let their' married children go. That newlywed should be fine because they've learned from you. You have probably taught them well. If you haven't it's too late to start over. Remember if they have learned, there is an excellent chance that they will make it over the long haul. Perhaps a few of the day-to-day things will not prove to be particularly remarkable, but everything will even out! We will teach more about parenting principles in Chapters 15 through 18.

However, when we are dealing with our grown offspring, separation from the nest is very delicate. We do not suggest that there be a radical departure from the child/parent relationship, but rather there should be a shifting in the relationship. Your parents will always be your parents and should be respected as such. Parents will usually have a wealth of experience, and a lot of wisdom forged out of that crucible of experience. But parents need even more of another kind of wisdom. Wisdom to know when to stop short of giving that advice; and a wisdom to share advice when sought, but not to get hurt, angry, or frustrated if the couple decides to do otherwise. *"I told you what to do, but you don't listen . . ." "If your head wasn't so hard . . ." "Go-ahead do your own thing; don't bother to ask me;"* are not statements that any parent should hurl at their grown married people. Remember advice provides an option, not a commandment. Newlyweds should not just throw away this valuable source of wisdom either. Don't be afraid to consult your parents for expanded options, but let everyone know that the final decisions are your responsibility. It is the God-given right of the husband/ wife team to make final decisions.

Some couples have taken the separation from their parents-clause to an extreme only to hurt themselves. They want to do everything on their own. It's far better to remember that there's no need to reinvent the wheel. If you can take the wheel and improve on it we call that progress. To reinvent, actually, wastes precious resources. In the realm of history, they say, *"That a man, who ignores history is doomed to repeat it."*

Another supporting principle to keep in mind is that the Bible teaches that **rebellion** is in the same category as **witchcraft**. If a couple chooses to ignore good sound wisdom from their parents solely because they are rebelling against their parents they are asking for trouble. This reminds me of the guy who refused to slow down at a police officer's instructions because he, *"disliked all cops,"* only to find out that the officer was trying to tell him that the bridge ahead was out. Testing his swimming skills at that time was totally unnecessary. Then there was Parsa who was so angry with her father because he felt that she was too young to marry and that she did not know the guy well enough to make that serious decision. Because of her anger she made a vow to go against every rule her father had ever made. She thought that she was paying him back, but what she was doing in the old colloquial expression was *"cracking her own neck."* There is certainly no pun intended but her husband turned out to be mentally and physically abusive. What a terrible price to pay for a rebellious heart. Then after all was said and done the marriage fell apart anyway. Parsa was reluctant but had to return to her parents because the man that she chose to trust too early devastated her.

Let's look at some of the principles discussed in these two Leaving chapters: The first principle in the scriptural formula for marriage is that each partner must leave father and mother, which represents the former family structure, in order to begin building and establishing a new family structure. There seem to be seven implications growing out of the leaving principle to help make stronger marriages.

1. Leaving home often involves the dissolving of preconceived negative notions and biases that interfere with sound discoveries of new strengths.
2. Old relationships must be redefined and accommodated in light of the new marriage alignment between husband and wife.
3. Often close friends need to be guided into a comfortable place of love that is not intrusive, yet is meaningful in a different way than the former attachments.
4. Leaving the parental nest does not mean loving less; it simply means redefining roles.

    a.   Now that I am married I'm not called upon to love my 'parents less, *but their involvement in our affairs as a couple changes.*

    b.   Neither of us (*in principle*) is directly answerable or accountable to our parents *for how we run our married lives.

3.   Leaving by public declaration seems to carry with it a strong implication for success. Marriage should not be a secret arrangement.

4.   Leaving home (a dividing of the new family unit away from former parental directed units) seems to be another strong implication for success.

5.   A legal marriage (performed according to the customs and traditions of one's society) is a mandate for the blessings of God to follow.

---

* **Of course, there are exceptions to any rule: Tina's life was saved when her parents stepped in and forced her to get medical attention for a deep cough that she was experiencing. The cough had persisted for over a month and Tina kept saying it was nothing even though she was coughing up blood. Her husband Herman trusted his wife's judgment. *"I'm sure Tina knows her own body well enough to know when something is really wrong,"* he said. Tina's mom got fed up one day after hearing her daughter hacking on the phone. She collected her husband and drove straight over to her ailing daughter's house.**

    ***"You are going out of here to a hospital this day young woman,"* as she snatched a jacket, threw it around her and pushed her into the car. The doctors discovered that Tina was about to go into advanced stages of pneumonia. Another day's delay and they might not have been able to save her.**

CHAPTER 7

THE CLEAVING FACTOR

Now let's look at the second leg of the marriage triangle. Cleaving is an old word hardly used anymore. Generally speaking, it is kind of like describing what glue does as it holds or sticks things together. Cleaving in a scriptural sense carries with it a deeper meaning than just holding or sticking to something. It actually means in the physical/ emotional sense, a clinging to, with a great desperation.

Once I heard a story about a man who not only was unable to swim, but was also actually terrified by any large body of water. I'm not sure how but someone convinced him to get on a big cruise ship to go sailing. The story goes that as he stood at the rail looking at the great sea before him the ship suddenly pitched and the man fell over the rail into the sea. Fortunately someone saw him fall and quickly threw him a life ring attached to a rope. *"Grab the ring,"* they screamed but the ring sailed out beyond him and he could not move toward it. Even though he could not reach the ring the rope was just over his head and he made one desperate successful lunge to grab it. *"Hold on,"* they again screamed, as they pulled him up to safety. It was an hour later when they were finally able to get the rope out of his hands. Those nearby claimed that his fingerprints were impressed in that rope. That man was desperate to live. This second leg of the triangular plan forces marriage partners to cleave to each other in a type of desperation. Walter Trobisch helps us understand that the cleaving process is actually the loving process.

For me, love is almost always understood as an action word. Love demands a grasping, clutching, weaving, knitting, binding action. In fact as an artist it reminds me of painting in a collage-like method. There are two main ingredients in a collage: paper and glue. The trick in doing a professional collage is to work paper and glue back and forth with a brushing method to eliminate all the space and air between the elements. This is done in order to create a finished product that cannot be separated because paper, picture and glue have become one.

A marriage needs love to survive and thrive. In our country we use the word love in several ways. I love ice cream. I love my dog. I love my' mom. I love my car. I love my wife. All of the above we use as legitimate statements, but all have a different connotation to the meaning. Doctor Ed Wheat says that there are actually five Greek words that better describe love: Epithumia, Eros, Storge, Phileo, and Agape. Epithumia is usually translated as lust, but is also used positively as a very strong physical desire. Christians might feel a little intimidated because of our teachings about modesty, however there is that part of us that is physically attracted to our' spouse in a hot, passionate, sexual way that goes far beyond mere attraction. So, we may enjoy Epithumia as a passionate desire, positive and blessed by God in every way!

Eros the second word he uses is more familiar to us. Eros is romantic love. It is the hearts and flowers; the silly little lighthearted moments of expressed love. Candlelight dinners, moonlight walks, love letters, hot tubs and the like are things that help us feel loved, or set the mood for more romance. Secondly, Eros is like the oil that makes the machinery run smoothly. Without this factor the parts are all there, but making them work without lubrication causes friction. Friction in machinery will cause negative heat; which in turn will cause the parts to wear out before time, or seize up. I once had an old Volkswagen with an engine that seized up. It would not move. I found through an acquaintance about the only mechanic who knew how to unfreeze that car. The problem was that the previous owner had neglected the lubrication system. So, Eros the romantic form of love must lubricate the love systems.

The word Storge, the third Greek word may not be familiar but it means basically, *"place of comfort."* It is like coming home from work and removing your shoes for some slippers, or just plain bare feet. You are at home; you are in a place of comfort. When you love someone, you, must make a place of comfort for him or her, a place of non-competition. And have you ever known a couple that seems to always compete with each other? Or, where one insisted on dominating the other person's space? Then I'm afraid you know some folks with the potential for marital troubles! In the marketplace I'm a competitor but that is only for outside of the home. Inside we must find ways of maintaining a place of peace that relaxes and comforts both partners.

The Storge relationship in a marriage effects both the romantic and the communication elements of the partnership. Plus, I just feel better about working with someone whom I feel is not out to produce a lot of stress in my life. I also must not be a producer of stress in their life either. Element number four Phile'o is the friendship element in the relationship. Married folk just ought to develop the closeness of best friends. That just seems to be a natural to me but I've observed over the years couples that develop great friendships outside of their marriage and neglect that all-important development between the partners.

Henrietta spent more time on the phone with Paula developing a spiritual bonding than with her husband Casper. The two ladies grew so close that they claimed to feel each other's pains. Soon Henrietta lost interest in her husband as they drifted apart. Little wonder; she never spent any time exploring and developing, or even communicating with the mind/heart of the one closest to her. Their marriage predictably broke up, not just because of a lack of Phile'o, but it certainly contributed to their internal problems. In his list Dr. Wheat's fifth element of love is called Agape. This is probably a familiar Christian statement of how God loves us. He loves us because He loves us! It has nothing to do with our face, how tall or short we are, what our weight is, or anything else. He loves us because He loves us. Our intellect or absence of intellect has nothing to do with His love for us. Money, fame, popularity has nothing to do with His love. He just loves us because He loves us!

Notice if you will, that Agape' love differs from the other five elements listed. The first four in the list are all reciprocal. *"If you do thus and so, I'll do thus and so." "Be my best friend, and I'll be your best friend." "Make it comfortable for me, and I'll do the same for you." "I'm going to romance you because I want the same in return." "I'm hot for your body, and I want you to be hot for mine."* All of the above are pretty much based on an expected return.

Agape actually says, *"I love you because I choose to love you." "In fact, you cannot make me not love you."* Listen, that last statement sounds like poor English usage, but the theology of it is very strong when you understand how God loves us. ***He chooses to love us, without condition!***

A marriage that has a strong commitment clause is far more likely to stand the test of time. Haven't you seen couples that cling to each other get even stronger as they get older? Surprisingly, there have been some film and stage actors and actresses that seem to be inseparable. The late Ozzie Davis and his widow Ruby Dee, and the late husband and widowed wife team of Hume Cronyn and Jessica Tandy come to mind. The flower of their youth had obviously faded from Ozzie and Ruby but their devotion and commitment to each other painted an even greater picture of love increasing. This is so rewarding to this observer in contrast to the expected 'Hollywood types', that seem not to have marriages as much as they have collections.

It is sad to see the Elizabeth Taylors of this world who have confused and abused the marriage bed so much that they end up with nothing in the golden years of their lives. In contrast to the emptiness and sadness viewed by those who can only boast of their collections, we could see the fire and passion when the late Ozzie Davis and his widow Ruby Dee were interviewed. Their love really showed! There was a pretty obvious agape connection working. We can also see it in the fiery eyes of former First Lady Nancy Reagan when she spoke of her late *"Ronnie,"* who suffered with Alzheimer's. There's a story out there about our former president out for walk accompanied by the Secret Service. He was clearly ailing from his illness when suddenly he turned and reached for the latch of an unfamiliar gate. Letting himself in he began to pick a flower. *"Mr. President,"* the startled agent exclaimed, *"This is not our home."* *"Oh, I know,"* said Mr. Reagan, *"I just wanted to take my love a flower."* Even though he was judged to be mostly locked in a private world, for just one precious moment he had returned to the love of his life. The embers of their love burned brightly in both of their hearts!

Love is certainly a choice. It has little to do with one's physical appearance, academic ability, age or station in life. Once that choice is made it should be made for life. It should not be made with *"If"* clauses. *"I will love you **if** you keep your beauty." "I will love you as long as I can admire your mind." "I will love you as long as you are on top of the heap."* It is pitiful that so many couples marry today with only a partial commitment to stay married. There's a marvelous passage of scripture that says, *"love is as strong as death." We know that death is not reversible in this life!* There are now some new terminologies cropping up: *"Starter marriages"* and *"Trial marriages"*. The meaning that I am hearing is that these are marriages that only last up to five years. More often it is expected to last about three years not to exceed five years. Common among these failed marriages is the feeling that they sort of take the first time as a trial balloon in order to do better, the next time around. Apparently, these marriages are not even expected to last. What kind of system promotes a failure syndrome as a hopeless model? **How can you expect to go somewhere, *when nowhere is the goal?***

Perhaps the starter marriage terminology came with the housing trend of new couples buying starter houses. Couples buy a small house not intending to stay long, but this is an investment. This is merely an investment ploy to gain equity for the eventual purchase of a larger house to come.

Remember agape love says, *"I love you because I choose to love you." **"In fact, you cannot make me not love you."*** Remember this statement is poor English usage, but very strong theology when you understand how God loves us. ***He chooses to love us, whether we deserve it or not!***

CHAPTER 8

GREASE-PAINT AND CEREMONY

THE CRACK AND zip of the new state of the art cameras, the rising hum of the otherwise reverent crowd, signaled the end of the ceremony. This was the wedding of the decade. There were multiple groomsmen decked out in designer tuxedos in compliment to a bevy of beautiful bridesmaids. The happy couple at this point is whisked off into the sunset. They have been properly arranged in a long chauffeur driven limousine, followed by a line of freshly washed cars, all with blaring horns announcing the launching of another nuptial ship.

The reception that follows is one spectacular event! Invited guests are treated to fancy little hors d'oeuvre as they walk through the doors of a plush private club, with distant sounds of an excellent live band. There is the usual reception line with the handsome Groomsmen and lovely ladies, all eager to shake hands with the arriving guests passing onto the great banquet dinner. Later, when all the guests are seated, the wedding party comes in. Each couple is introduced to the smiles and approving nods, and applause of friends and well wishers. Then comes the crowning moment. 'Mr. and Mrs. Just Got Married', float through to their seats of honor. *"Beautiful"*, you think, *"Simply beautiful"!* And certainly they are beautiful.

The above is a put-together illustration, but I wonder how many times a year this similar scene is repeated? Sometimes it may not be as elaborate as our description here, but none the less exciting.

One could think with all of this marvelous show of sending off, that our couple would live happily ever after. If this were a fairy tale, I'm sure they would, but after the dream, comes the blatant, stark reality. I have two nagging problems with these all too common repeating scenes. One is just plain economics; the other I'll call, *"Trip planning"*.

JUST PLAIN ECONOMICS

Big halls, fancy foods, and chauffeur driven limousines all cost big bucks these days. Tradition has called for the bride-to- be, and her family (usually that means her father) to bare most of the expense of the wedding. That same tradition saw the groom paying for the rings, and those few expenses relating to himself and his groomsmen. These expenses most likely are his attire and flowers for the men. He in addition, is responsible for paying the minister for performing the ceremony. (Don't forget that the minister is worthy of his fee. Even if he or she is your pastor, it is an extra demand on his or her time.) When you add it up, the bride's expenses under the Historical/ traditional system, far outweigh the groom's cash output. Someone once said, *"It was alright for the bride to pay now because for the rest of his life the man would be paying"*. I am glad however, that there seems to be a beginning trend towards sharing the wedding cost. I admire young men who are thoughtful enough to even consider helping the bride's family with these bills that have been traditionally/ historically thought of as belonging to her, and her family.

In reality, both people are involved in a wedding. Why not share the expense and the planning. This should be a great time of learning and sharing. Brides beware of the emerging 'new man' of our times. He is surely more sensitive and alert. He is also more opinionated about detail things. Unlike his older counter-part, he is now likely to express his views, likes, and dislikes. If he is going to invest, he is going to want to have input. I've experienced planning sessions where the man has been involved in what colors he thinks are appropriate, etc. These things did not take place a few decades ago. But think about it this way: the bottom line here is if they cannot plan together at this great launching of their nuptial vows, how then can they expect to live successfully together as husband and wife? A successful marriage is one continuing system of planning together.

Weddings are running in the multi-thousands of dollars. But where is the money going? Now every father ought to be proud of his daughter. If she has been a loving and sweet girl there is little wonder at wanting to show her off to the world. Yet just how much of that is done in appreciation, and praise; and how much is done under the pressure of keeping up with some image? I'm afraid that even in the Christian community where conservative values of good stewardship are encouraged we have slipped drastically. We now seem to promote the idea of weddings being as large as possible. Not too many years ago there was a famous preacher who threw one gigantic wedding ceremony. The world had to stop and view this one. Some speculated that it cost her almost a half of a million dollars or more. Sorry to say, I don't think it was quite a year later when they again made headlines as they headed for a nasty divorce.

The size of the wedding does not guarantee the success of the marriage. In fact, it sometimes causes a reversal. We know that one of the factors effecting marriage in a negative way, is that of fighting over finance. The wedding bills sometimes leave a deep scar on what should have been happy memories. People, who can't afford show-place weddings, are now being encouraged to act out a lie. They often agree to spend money they don't have. What should be a heart—warming, pleasant experience for lovers setting out on a lifetime journey, is often a financial nightmare! A nightmare lasting sometimes for years and many payments to come.

I am not suggesting that couples ship off to their local justice of the peace to avoid expenses. To the contrary, I think it is wonderful when a couple gets married in the church. Especially if they are a part of that church. Sometimes because of the numbers of relatives and friends their particular church may not be able to hold the expected crowd. Some have even desired to rent an exotic place to hold their wedding or/ and reception in. If you want it and can really afford it then do it. On the other hand, why then does this have to run some people to the 'Poor house'? The answer is that it does not! With some very careful planning, free from a lot of outside pressures, expenses can be held down. When we are pressured by what other people think, feel, and want, we may limit our own creativity and certainly, stretch our limited capacity.

Lance and Edith were planning to have a small reception following their marriage ceremony. They had pretty much lost interest in their old friends after joining the church. They enjoyed the fresh direction of the church family. Edith had been on her own away from her family for years. Lance had spent several years in the military. Together they did not have much money so they wanted to keep everything simple.

The big rub came when Lances' family, who were very much into the party crowd, could not understand why the couple was not interested in having a big reception bash. To them the only way you could have a good time was to have a house full of available liquor. His family was against the church, and its' different drum beat.

Edith planned a simple church reception. Instead of the traditional chicken salad dinner, which had been the norm for a while they decided to have a fruit bowl reception. Punch, cake, and fresh sliced fruit in baskets cut from hollowed out watermelon. This was all to be arranged on a long table display. Guests would serve themselves, buffet style.

Just before the wedding, Lance's family announced that they had it all together. Following the wedding, the couple was expected to come to his relatives' home for an after party. Lance and Edith were very reluctant to go to this after party. The couple felt that a lot would go on that was against their beliefs. I was asked my opinion. Since they did not have to invest any money into a life style they no longer believed in, the solution seemed fairly simple. I saw nothing wrong with them putting in an, appearance and leaving at an appropriate time. After all, even if they did not agree with these relatives, a show of respect and appreciation for them even caring was in order. On the other hand, had these relatives insisted on the couple being financially responsible for this activity, there would be grounds for a flat out refusal. You must take control of what you want.

Let's face the facts. Your family, friends, church members, neighbors, or anyone else who counts, do not care how big, or small you make your wedding, as long as they don't have to pay for it. I've attended lawn receptions, hall receptions, and church receptions. Add to that private club receptions, home receptions, etc. In no case did I refuse to go because of what it was costing the couple. It's your reception. If I care about you, you could have it in a parking lot, which was done, and I would come. Your wedding-your reception is for you. Make it suitable for you. Just remember to plan within your means.

What about your financial means? Is there a limit? Can you over do it, or under do it? In the case of Adam and Gwen in chapter four there was no question that their wedding was excessive and beyond their ability. Gwen's folks were well to do; and she, a professional woman having worked a number of years, had saved a goodly sum. Adam was a nighttime student who worked at a low paying full-time day position. He had little or no savings. For Gwen and her parents to go out and plan the wedding social event of the decade was neither fair, nor good planning. Adam was forced from day one to live a life style that he could not succeed at.

Entering into marriage in hock up to the gills is certainly not my best recommendation! Make your wedding plans based on your own abilities, expectations, and reasonable objectives. Don't waste everything on the grease paint.

THERE IS A NEW TYPE BEING CONSIDERED

Well actually, it is no longer new. I've been aware of it for almost two Decades. It is the "Runaway wedding", or that's what I'll call it. Instead of the traditional wedding held in a local church, hall etc. the couple plans to have their wedding take place in one of the islands abroad. Believe it or not this seems to be a less expensive way to have a wedding. Now there are the normal charges and expenses of the wedding attire, the added costs of the plane tickets, but here's where the savings begin to add up. The bride and the groom virtually get their way paid by loading up the hotel with wedding party and other invited guests. The bridal couple does not have to pay for big reception. First of all how many friends and relatives are going to spend the money to go abroad? So, the numbers are cut down to begin with. The couple can afford to go with light refreshments, etc. instead of a huge feast, with its decorations, hall rentals and a menagerie of the other expenses designed to please those coming to the festivities. So, I am told that these wedding packages have become quite competitive contrasting traditional expenses.

One extra bonus that might be considered is that aunt Mabel is not likely to drag a Crockpot over to the Caribbean islands, and might just decide to give some money to avoid the inconvenience of it all.

GOING SOMEWHERE?????

You know I almost forgot to talk about going somewhere. Yes, I mean the honeymoon. I know everyone wants to go to some exotic place to make a wonderful memory. The problem with that is, unless you have saved a pretty good bundle you need to think this through very carefully. Many couples fly the friendly skies to somewhere they really can't afford. Sometimes these decisions are made to impress others. I wonder how impressive it is to have to call up a friend to borrow money to complete the dream that's about to turn into a nightmare? If you can go to Aruba, or Santa Domingo, etc. because of a well-planned package do it heartily my friend. But if it is going to strain your resources you might just want to think about going somewhere affordable now, and planning for the more expensive trip later.

EXPECTING GIFTS

I thought that I would devote some space and attention to someone's question, *"What's a wedding without gifts"?* I heard about a salty bride who when pelted with some thrown rice at their wedding shouted, *"You folks better take that rice home and cook it!"* That is a rather sharp rebuke for a bride to make to her relatives and friends who are trying to celebrate her wedding, but basically, I agree. There should be a practical element to our actions. Throwing food is wasting precious resources. I have seen some weddings lately that threw bird seed instead of rice. I suppose that this newer practice is better because it potentially will feed some birds. Before buying a wedding gift we should be aware of a couple's needs. Many unthinkingly give fancy gadgets that have little to do with their real needs. Our gift choices should never be intended to impress onlookers. Evaluate the likely needs that you anticipate in the future. Dishes, cooking utensils, various appliances, towel-washcloth sets, bedding, cutting knives, eating ware, etc. are all practical items that will find great use by the newlyweds. Fancy gifts that do little are of little use and of questionable value in shaping the home of the new couple.

I remember when we got married that there was a lady from my wife's home town that sent to us a wedding gift of some used pots and pans. We thought it was a little unusual and kind of laughed, but were thankful anyway. Later on, we found ourselves extremely grateful. These pots and pans were to be the only such cooking utensils we would have for a long while. No one else had thought to give us pots and pans. We had so little money that new purchases for us were out of the question.

Now please, I am certainly not suggesting that anyone think of giving any used items to newlyweds. It was frankly a little embarrassing to us, and we were not just sure what was meant by it, especially since this lady did not have a financial problem. We finally concluded that she had only good intentions. Funny enough, as I look back, it is about the only wedding gift I remember receiving. It certainly fit the need. This may serve as a good example for you as a gift giver. Plan with the future in mind. What will they remember 15, or 20 years from now?

I understand that some wise mothers now distribute gift needs lists to family and friends along with the invitations. I hope in doing this that they are listing sound needs for the present and near future. I'm sure that there would be those who would disagree with me if I were to suggest that fine crystal and display china are more luxury items than basic needs. These good folk would argue that these are once in a life- time items and that it is unlikely to be many other times in the life of this couple to receive such expensive gifts. They would further offer that these kinds of gift items increase in value. The price paid now would escalate far beyond current price. Surprisingly, I agree with all of the above. Yet I feel that time is *now* when needs are more crucial to their existence. We should lean more toward the practical. If we don't do all we can to help this marriage in the beginning; we may never have to worry about an increase in item value. Then, on the other hand, I'm not sure after thinking about it that all this feeling comes from gut-level only.

Experience in working with young couples has shown me that any legitimate means of helping the couple financially is, after all, a genuine help! The financial pressures are at their greatest at the beginning of the marriage. To be sure these pressures usually continue throughout the marriage, but I suppose after a while one gets somewhat more used to them. Never comfortable with them you understand—just used to them! The reason I picture them as being more crucial in the beginning, when in fact, they are always going to be troublesome, is that in the beginning, usually neither party has had any real experience in this area. Lack of finance has buried many couples. The death nail was inserted from day one. If you, dear couple, are fortunate enough to receive wedding gifts in cash, why not consider depositing all such funds into a prearranged joint savings account? Don't plan to spend this money! And for goodness sake, don't plan to pay off wedding bills with it! If you don't make big wedding expenses, you won't have big bills to pay off.

Well over two decades ago I listened intently to Grace, a proud mother whose last daughter was about to marry. She explained to me an elaborate plan for nuptial finance. I confess that it was so intricate that I did not get all of it. But here is what I remember. It seems that they figured the wedding was going to cost them approximately $5-$6,000. Given twenty years back that was quite a figure. Today it would have probably been about twelve to maybe fifteen grand.

This figure of twenty years ago included the dress, the cake, the wedding hall, and the caterers. I exclaimed, having at that time no experience with the financial end, that it seemed awfully high to me. Grace assured me that they had cut out a sizable portion of the fat. Further, she was delighted that her plan would see the money they put out, come back. She knew that several of the relatives were planning to give large financial gifts. She speculated further that the average guest would be giving either gifts of cash, or items having cash value. They had prearranged with several national department stores; all having computerized gift lists. You could call in Chicago to see what had already been selected from the couples needs list in Boston. It would tell you what was left to choose from. This way, duplicate irons, toasters, etc. would not likely happen. Should someone not consult these stores and buy a duplicate iron, or coffeepot, that was all right. Grace and daughter planned to gather certain extra items to take back to the stores for refunds. This money would, of course, be added to the other gift money. By the time she finished sharing this information with me, I was convinced that she had spent a lot of time developing this plan, and that she was convinced that it would work. I had my own misgivings, chiefly because I had no background with this kind of thing. Today it is the norm to have a Bridal Registry program.

There was one very important thing that was established in my mind from that conversation; the important role the bride's mother could play in arranging the wedding matters. I will always appreciate Grace for her planning skills.

Concern for security has become an element that looks like it will always be with us. I had the feeling though, that Grace would not see one wedding present lost or unaccounted for. When I was very young, I remember attending receptions in homes where the gifts were displayed unattended in a bedroom. You cannot do that today. Someone must be assigned to secure the gifts. The bride's mother should do the assigning where possible. I also learned that all cards and gifts envelopes containing money, should be placed in the hands of the brides' mother, or in some rare case, her designate. Even those envelopes placed personally in the bride's hands, should be given quickly to mom. Common sense suggests to us that the tired, excited, nervous bride's attention is on her new husband. It is not the time when a brand new wife's practical business sense, is in full operation.

Well, I might as well turn from these matters and attack the, *"Sacred cow."* It may not make me very popular, but one of the biggest areas of wedding waste is found in the wedding attire. Everyone wants to see how the couple looks on their wedding day. It is truly amazing how much money is spent on one-time garments. I once heard about someone experimenting with paper throwaway clothing. If anyone ever develops a one-time paper wedding gown that has the look and feel of an expensive wedding cloth, that person's financial worries are over! I have a cousin who is a fashion designer specializing in bridal fashions. One interesting creation of hers features a convertible gown. After the wedding ceremony, the dress can be prepared for the reception. The bridal train and some of the lower areas are removed to reveal a party dress. This party dress can at least be used again for another formal or semiformal occasion. It will work in theory, as long as the lady does not plan to change sizes.

Another alternative toward the practical is the makeover. Sometimes older relatives have gowns that have been preserved and are in good shape. Sonia found her grandmother's dress in the attic. She found a good seamstress who reworked the dress to fit her. The results were a little more expensive than she thought, but beautiful. It still did not cost anywhere near the cost of a new gown. It is certainly a little less expensive than getting a seamstress to make the gown from scratch. Sometimes if the bride to be puts on a real search she may find some bargains in the larger bridal shops. Bargains and discounts sometime occur because of dress age, soil, display models, or other reasons that the managers feel that they cannot sell at full price.

Some bridal companies now feature a plan for the brides to get back a part, or all of their gown price. This plan is based on her bridesmaids purchasing their dresses and accessories from that company. If they do that for the bride, you can be sure that the same kind of arrangement is possible for the groom. It does help ease the financial pressure for the couple, but it is kind of using one's friends.

I'm afraid in the area of gown expenses I'm not too helpful. I do think a bride needs to look at as many options as she can. However, when it comes to the groom, I offer my most radical suggestion on the subject. I would rather see the groom invest his money in something that will net him the greatest return.

Renting a tux is the norm, but buying a good, up to date suit is far more practical. He will get years of wear out of that suit. The rented tux goes back in the morning! A terrific looking black suit seems to be the most versatile, but they've done a lot with various shades of gray. White suits are beautiful, but one needs to consider if it can be worn practically afterward. It may seem a bold step from tradition, but later, the couple will see it as a good investment. The groomsmen will certainly appreciate it following the wedding when they see the money they've spent as a usable investment. Several years ago, I ran into a great investment. A relative in business said that there was a shop for men across the street that was having a sidewalk sale. She said they had some white formal suits, and that she asked the man, to hold my size. When I got there, I found the tux to be all she said it was. For under twenty-five dollars, I walked away with a bran new formal tuxedo. It needed a little cleaning because it had become shop-worn. I then went to a formal shop and purchased a white cummerbund that had been retired from the rental pool. The outfit was rounded out with a white bow tie. This small investment certainly paid off for many years. I finally retired this investment after my body decided to change to a more popular size. Well anyway that's one way to put it. We pass this information along to point out that there are alternatives out there that could prove to be long range bargains. If you just have to have a tux, why not check out a purchase from the rental pool. You may, in years later, have to have lapels narrowed, a bit let out, etc., but I'm sure you'll get some good mileage before then. I realize that what I've suggested is a bold departure from the current trend. Yet what I am looking at is the unwise use of limited funds. I don't suggest that we budget all the fun out of the wedding. I merely lobby for putting sanity into the spending practices.

In a survey done several years ago by my semester III class in *'Marriage and Family'*, conflicts in finance emerged as the third highest cause of problems in the marriages surveyed. I believe this survey to be a valid slice of life in our American society. In a large percentage of the marriage counseling sessions that I do this again seems to surface as a major cause of conflict.

I need to make a financial connection, between couples going to the altar and how many of these marriages fare financially down the road. Here is a type of statement that's heard in my office: *"Carl takes no interest, in paying bills. All the debts are on me, and he doesn't even want to hear about them. I feel pressured, betrayed, and just plain tired of it."* Later in the session the husband retorts, *"Well Cathy wants everything her way. She goes around spending all the money, and I'm sure that's just how she wants it!"* How much of that started while leading up to the altar?

It is here that we should talk about disenfranchising. In human beings there seems to be a need for ownership in something that life has to offer. If not total ownership, we need to see ourselves as significant investors. All kinds of experiments have been done in human behavior demonstrating our' progress in situations where one feels a part, as opposed to when one feels, left out. My speculation is that even worse is to have once been an integral part, and then to be stripped of that part. If the man is completely left out in putting together the wedding ceremony, etc. is there any guarantee that he will feel like coming back fully into all of the financial decisions during the marital journey? Disenfranchising is a real factor. Men do not easily heal from being ignored. It is part of that unique male mechanism. Don't just ignore it. But rather learn to work with it. Approach it as a joint blessing!

GOOD TRIP PLANNING IS FOR THE WISE

The very first thing that a couple can really plan together before they actually, get married, is the wedding. It is here that they can learn to work together. In all of your married life, you will be involved in planning, hopefully together. If the male in the relationship either gives away, or is robbed, of his involvement, it will pay off in later frustrations, and trouble. If here, before it even begins, he learns to bow out, he might just decide to continue this pattern. It will to him seem easier. He doesn't have to listen to a lot of chatter.

She, on the other hand, might find it very comfortable in the beginning to take on the role of the lone decision-maker. After all she does not have to listen to his steady stream of objections. The problem here is that several miles down the road they will both discover that it doesn't work that way! Things often begun become pattern makers for a future run. When a person feels that his thoughts, his experience, and his involvement are appreciated and necessary, he will likely give full cooperation. The person has a stake, or franchise in the project. With ownership, or investment comes a sense of pride. Take that away, or fail to develop it and the results are feelings of disenfranchisement, or loss of worthiness.

I knew of a couple that experienced serious problems because one of the spouses took over the full control of everything. The other spouse felt left out and disenfranchised, causing after a while, deep emotional/mental problems. When a decision had to be made, it was made for the nonvoting spouse. This was clothing, house furnishings, car, and even friends, to a certain degree. Little wonder that a spouse treated this way may retreat into a world of his or her own. This disenfranchised spouse became more and more withdrawn, eventually causing outsiders to fear for the person's mental health.

Equal ownership in the decision-making process is vital to the success of the marriage. This process of management should begin development in the engagement period. Dating and engaged couples should develop a communication habit. Why habit? Habit, because good communication between close people does not reside in the area of ability alone. Good communication is found more so in the area of our willingness. Couple that willingness and skill with lots of practice. Remember this is to be a lifetime journey.

Many people have the ability to communicate extremely well, but just flat out refuse to do so. Use this dating period in your life to begin, and to develop this process that must follow you into the marriage and then continue to build throughout.

Let's be honest, a partner in the dating or engagement period, who refuses to share verbally, is not likely to become a talking Magpie in a marriage relationship. *What you are to become, you must begin to be.* One of the helpful things that a couple might do as they begin planning for the big day is to visit their local library. You will find several good books on how it is done. Information on ceremony, traditions, format, and process can be found in your local Christian bookstore. Another helpful resource is in talking to persons that have been through it scores of times, such as wedding coordinators, pastors, and others. Surely there is great information on the internet, but I always caution that any information regardless the source must be weighed carefully. It being on the internet or in a book does not necessarily validate it. Pray your way through the maze.

Then there are other persons who might not have been involved in the actual wedding planning, but by the nature of their job they may be able to make helpful input. I'm sure a church secretary can share some insight from the business side of what happens church-wise during a wedding. Are special arrangements needed for older relatives, and guests? What is to be done with large gifts that are brought to the church that must eventually be taken to the reception area? Can security be provided in any way? Will you be using the regular church ushers, or honorary ushers who may not be familiar with the physical plant? What fees are expected and by whom? What times should be arranged for rehearsal night, and the actual wedding. People usually set a time for folk to gather, but is there a leaving time? Are staff persons just expected to wait around for hours until the last guest decides to leave? These are questions that the church secretary might be helpful in answering.

Another excellent resource person is the church custodian. This person might well have a story to tell. I'm sure it would be helpful to suggest how many chairs and tables you estimate are needed if the reception is to be held at the church. What guide lines for trash disposal should be followed? Are any special details needed? What about physical arrangements, such as altarpieces, flowers, candles, public address system, etc.? Do not just assume that someone will take care of it. In fact, it might be better to assume that someone will not! I was officiating in a recent wedding that was held in a rented church. Their system was really great. Everything needed could be checked on a special form. This was done months ahead of time. During the rehearsal, it was noted that the piano, which was kept locked and covered, had not been requested. The office was closed since this was a Friday evening. Fortunately, the custodian was in charge. What a helpful man! Even though the piano was overlooked he said, "I'll take care of it". Later it was discovered that an extra microphone and a step up platform, were also needed. There was fear that since these important items had not been pre-ordered that we would have to work around the needs? Again, the custodian came to the rescue. We soon found that in spite of the fancy order form, and well-planned church system, this man was in charge. To respect him, was the key to the smooth running of this wedding ceremony?

A good wedding should come as a result of good planning. Good planning should include each phase of the wedding, from start to finish. When you have worked out your plan begin communicating early with each participant just what his, or her role is, and what your expectations are. If you tell people fully up front, the hope is that they will have enough time to see if they can fit in and be of help.

Tress readily agreed to be Ada's Maid of honor. She was anxious to do it. In accepting, she was unaware that she'd be responsible for purchasing her dress, and the accessories. Tress was between jobs and had to save every bit of money she had. The girls seemingly never talked about the surrounding financial conditions involved, until well into the final count-down. Ada thought that her maid of honor knew what was expected. Tress, on the other hand having never been in a wedding, thought that the expenses were paid for by the bride. This kind of confusion could have been avoided if when the assignment was made, full disclosure of all obligations were also made. The person accepting could just as easily decline the position if they could not live up to the expectations. This would include not only commitments to finances, but various time tasks as well.

My observations are: that when developing a plan, one should try to make things as economical as possible. You will also need to plan for inconveniences and the economy of time. Convenience and time are as important to consider as the dollar amount. You will want to strive for a good balance. I remember in a non-marriage related incident, some of my Aunts poking fun at my grandfather one day. It seems he had found a gasoline station that sold gas a few cents cheaper than all the others. He delighted in filling up his car with these newfound savings. The joke came in when one of the daughters pointed out *"Daddy, it may be a few cents cheaper, but you have to go all the way to New Jersey to get it! Just think about the bridge tolls, and the extra mileage."* You see he had thought about saving on the price of the fuel, but failed to consider the other factors. Strive for a balance as you plan. Don't be penny wise, and pound-foolish.

Another observation is, that most, *Best Men*, have very little understanding of what they should be doing. So it is that much of what should be done either goes undone, or is sandwiched in somehow. Plan a wedding day before hand. Don't just make it up as the day unfolds. It would be wise to involve the *Best Man* in the planning early on. And of course a review as the day nears is in order. Also, it would not hurt to send out commitment notes to the other *Groomsmen* stating what their job assignments are. Simply stated, the *Best Man* should attend to the needs of the groom relating to the wedding day. Often he is the one that helps coordinate the selections, etc. He should be the one picking up, and returning the rented garments *for all the men* of the wedding party. *A simple fact often forgotten: The Groom* is usually off on his honeymoon by Monday morning when his rented wedding clothes must be back, along with the others.

Jumping back to the wedding day, let me say emphatically, that the groom should never be running around town picking up tuxes, driving people from the airport, and a hundred and one other things that some other responsible folk could do. Here are a few other duties for our best man. Most people are aware that the best man is expected to carry the bride's ring to the wedding altar for the groom. *But here is another often not known duty:* ***He should see to it that the marriage license is placed in the hands of the officiating clergy person prior to the ceremony.***

Some clergy persons insist that they have the license several days before the wedding. The best man should also be the one to get with the minister directly after the ceremony to make sure everything is signed and sealed. I always prefer to make the license delivery personally to the bride's mother, when possible. She already has the responsibility for holding all of the cards and cash gifts. These she will hold until they can sit down and properly tend to business. If money or important documents are placed in the hands of our couple, already over-excited by the events of the day, carelessness could easily follow.

The best man should be prepared to act as the groom's forerunner. There is an interesting parallel that comes to mind: That of John the baptizer who actually, heralded the coming of Jesus, the bridegroom of the church. John proved faithful in his task recognizing that he was not, *"that light,"* but prepared to hold fast until the coming of the one he represented. He was an excellent front man because he realized that as the groom appeared, his role was to decrease as the groom's increased. Yet notice that John continued to play a strong supportive role as he began to release his disciples to the authority of Jesus.

Just as a best man should be a functioning one, so should the bride's maid, and the matron of honor. There is a lot of up front work that has to be done before the wedding. The bride should not be ashamed to ask for help. Invitations have to be addressed and mailed, decorations, and furnishings have to be gathered, flowers arranged, and so much more. Use your ladies to help with as much as possible. That should be the nature of the honor. But so many times it seems to be strictly honorary. When I hear that this one just flew in from somewhere on the other side of the country in time for the ceremony I suspect that their role is simply honorary. Usually these persons have absolutely no idea of what's going on. The hope is that the measurements that were sent two, or three months ago, will still fit! Yet into town they come so close to wedding time that nothing in the way of service can be rendered. So close that if an extra pound or two has been added, they'll just have to hold it in because there's no time for the slightest of alterations.

There's another reason that I feel members of the wedding party coming from far distances should arrive at least a full day in advance. When people are coming in close to the time, think of the strain and stress it places on the couple. They are trying to coordinate their own lives, and schedules. Think of the added burden they will have of going for arriving guests, and the wedding-party. I recall a recent wedding being held in a town where neither of the couple lived. Everyone stayed in hotels kind of spread out. The airport that most of the folks coming to the wedding had to use was quite a distance. It was not an easy task coordinating. Just the arrivals alone was a major task. Add to that the check-ins, etc. The church was in another direction entirely. I marveled at the way this couple managed to put and keep things together. I'm sure that this is a skill that they took with them into their marriage. They actually did a great job, however I could not help thinking of the great strain it put on them. Because of this strain they could have easily slept their way through the whole honeymoon. I certainly hope not!

On the wedding day someone has to help the bride get dressed. Her make-up has to be special and just right. Her hair must be combed and teased, and pinned to perfection. The logical ones to help with this would be the bride's ladies. Our reason again for mentioning the above is that so often those carrying the titles are not those actually doing the work. I could compare it to the first years of our ministry when we raised a lot of our ministry funding by hosting an annual concert and banquet. Boy how we worked with that thing! Every detail had to be done. Nothing went beyond our touch. People always said they loved these annual events. This was pretty evident, because they would come the next year. There was one thing however that I never admitted; I never experienced the same joy my guests did. My body was so tired, and my mind so stressed out that I was more like a Zombie. I would always get through it with a hardy smile and cordial words because I was a pretty good actor in those days. But in reality, I knew what was on my dinner plate, for I planned it, but hardly tasted it. Over-work will spoil the joy! This should not be the plight of the bride and groom on this, the day of their nuptial launching. **So- choose carefully those who will serve you best!** Plan way ahead. I'm sorry to say this, but don't just choose someone because you started Jr. High School together and you haven't seen them for about six years. The reason for you all being out of touch is they moved to the West coast. Their plan is to arrive several hours ahead of the event. Just in time to throw on their garment. Yes, you love that person very much but will they in actuality be able to help you with your wedding plans? They are not even at the rehearsal and end up kind of awkwardly stumbling through. Is it really worth it; you must decide?

You will need help! The people in your wedding party should be helpers. Perhaps you could put up with maybe one honorary person but certainly not a hold group of them. Not if you really want this day to work well! In order to have a chance to look at what you have planned, if at all possible, have a dry run through to see if you can discover any hitches.

Recently I officiated for a wedding where the coordinator was obtained from the internet. We found out later that her references were a bit vague to put it mildly. Someone figured out that this was probably her first wedding. Now everyone has to start somewhere and that was not the major problem. In this particular wedding there were present several would be-coordinators plus myself who all had a lot of experience and a pretty good idea of what needed to be done. This was still not the problem because it was our friends who were marrying and we would not let this wedding fail. The problem was that no one liked the coordinator because she had a bad attitude. She pretended to know stuff that she clearly did not know and refused to let anyone help her. Girlfriend had a serious attitude! I think also if she could have begun developing a kind of relationship before meeting everyone the night of the rehearsal it would have gone smoother. I am sure that the only reason that the wedding party did not try to sabotage the wedding was for the great love they had for the couple. Because of the coordinator there were a lot of negative feelings and expressions of mutiny.

A wedding calls for so much work ahead of time. A wedding coordinator ought to be able to be helpful long before the rehearsal night when most of the wedding party is pressed into service. It bears repeating,

**CHOOSE CAREFULLY THOSE WHO
WILL SERVE YOU BEST!**

LOVE AND MARRIAGE FOR A LIFETIME

**Two books in one.
Let the journey continue.
*MARRIAGE Volume 2***

CHAPTER 1

AFTER YOU SAY I DO . . .

I HOPE BEFORE you said, *"Yes, I will"*, hoping to later on say at the altar, *"I do,"* you stopped and counted the cost! We opened this series with our first book LOVE FOR A LIFETIME, with an illustration of a great house being built. We asked, "Who begins to build a house without first taking a look at how much it is going to cost? Our church many years ago looked at a building project that was estimated at $150,000 to build. The architect then added a postscript to his estimate. He said that even though we were looking at a cost of $150,000 that day, by the time the project was finished (*in less than a year*) the cost would be more like $183,000. He figured in 'cost over-runs', additional labor, and material up-grades, etc.

Marriages are forged from the crucibles of life. When you said I am interested in saying, *"I do"*, I hope you examined all the factors you could think of. Each element of marriage has to be weighed against the backdrop of God's word, and that crucible we mentioned. What you see today in that person's character that you don't like is very unlikely to change tomorrow, or in quite a few tomorrows!

I love this quote from Judge Joan Barnes Perry-Stewart, *"Also … Do you think "marrying" and "marriage" are the same thing? If you are talking about working on and maintaining what you thought was going to be the blissful state of marriage, but are surprised to find it's not that much fun; there's no money, and occasionally small people throw up on you, then 'marriage' is your word. (Jamie, the guy from the beach that lives at my house, keeps talking about being "manacled together since The Battle of Agincourt." I'm not sure what he means.) 'Marrying' seems to be a process that culminates on a particular day that involves a cake and a big white dress. In my experience those were ultimately not interchangeable concepts. Gotta go! I'm making homemade bread and I forgot about it and now I'm getting ready to burn down the house. THAT, is called "marriage!" "LOL."* Thanks Joan, I got it!

I sat in my office preparing for a counseling session with a couple who was having some problems with authority, responsibility, respect, honor, and love. All of those major kinds of things, that cause marital breakdowns. I felt really helpless to bring them to a rallying point. I wanted to get them to come together and regroup. My custom has always been to ask God to lead in each counseling session. Only God can see beyond the surface of man's experience. Often one looks at a problem in a way that is contrary to the perception of the other partner. Someone said, in fact I believe it was my very wise mother, *"There are always three sides to every story: his side -her side, and the real side"*! Well only God knows the real side. So, I asked God, as usual, to reveal to me the real side, and to give me the handles to work with. It was here that God revealed the scriptural principle that I call **"The Shepherding Covenant"**.

I had been exposed all my life to Psalm twenty-three. Yet never did I know, or think, that there was any connection with marriage. Let's look at this favorite of Psalms in a new way. Please take a moment out to ask God to open your eyes, and your understanding, to see the truth of this important principle, as it relates to marriage. This is the antidote that will lead many warring couples from the brink of disaster.

Psalm twenty-three opens with the declarative statement: *"The Lord is my Shepherd . . ."* Scripture teaches us that Sarah called Abraham *'lord'.* An understanding of New Testament scriptures like Ephesians 5:22-24. Colossians 3:18, and 1 Peter 3:1 establish that the husband is placed, by God, in the role of family head. Actually, the Ephesians passage compares the relationship of the wife to the husband as, *"unto the lord",* (small *l*). Colossians helps us in understanding further the context of that statement by using, *"As it is fit in the Lord."* In our words we would say, *"Just as it would be fitting to the Lord".* Putting all of this together the understanding is that a wife should look to her husband as an under-lord of their family. *We are not in any way suggesting that the family head is superior—***just *responsible*!**

It should also be added at this point that while God holds him responsible as the head of the family, there is nowhere stated, or implied that the husband should make all of the decisions himself without the council of his wife. He is not family boss just the head. He is like the manager of a company. He does not own it. In fact Ephesians 5:21 gives balance by teaching that a husband and a wife must practice submitting, one to the other.

To make any major life decisions independent of either mate is to court certain disaster. Charles got trapped in a business scam that sent his financial base plummeting because he failed to listen to his wife's cautions. He felt she was being a little too spiritual minded in a simple supply and demand market. What he entered into did not just become a financial drain, but an unexplained heaviness that pressed upon his spirit. In another example of unwise decision making, Maybell decided to buy a new car without her husband's agreement. She felt that he was unable to understand the financial benefits she would gain by trading in her car of 5 or 6 years. She believed herself to be far superior to her husband in business. Maybell felt that Rob, on top of everything else, was chauvinistic, and mean. Perhaps he was all of that, and some more, but she violated a principle when she decided to ignore his objections altogether. She bought the car, and from that time on she placed herself under heavy financial bondage. Actually, she almost lost the car at one point, because she got seriously behind in her payments. Maybell was terrified about having to tell Rob what was really going on. She said that she didn't want to hear him say, *"I told you so"*. Yet my counsel was to do just that. *"Tell him"*, I told her. *"You cannot make a wrong right by continuing to do wrong"*. In so many marriages wrongs *are* done, but are never straightened out. It is like putting bad seeds in the ground hoping they really won't grow into weeds. On the street where my daughter and her husband and family live there is a tree that drops its' fruit after every spring. They look like grey grapes but if someone accidentally steps on one it produces a gross stink smell that's hard to imagine. Whoever in the world planted it there, right in front of someone's house? They really need to cut it down. However, do it long before spring comes!

In fact, I know enough about gardening to tell you weeds will probably grow faster and more persistent than your good plants. That's the nature of weeds and that's the nature of wrong stuff carelessly planted in a marriage. Disaster does not always come immediately on the heels of a one sided decision, but beware! A marriage cannot successfully grow from a one sided selfish perspective.

Being the head of the family does not mean that the man can, or should make every single decision. His job as head calls him to the responsibility of seeing that the best decision for a given situation is made. Many times this calls for his endorsement of her best judgment. In the case of major decisions however, final judgment, action, or sometimes reaction, should try to follow a joint commitment. I'm sure in every marriage there are those times (*hopefully only a few*) when the man must take the responsibility of making final judgment decisions. Let me tell you as a husband those times would really be painful for me. That's not the way for issues to be decided.

Please let the reader note: No decision made by the husband is final without the wife's right of appeal. Especially if it appears that decision was not made in good judgment, or in the best interest of the family.

The appeal process for a wife will be shared in a later chapter. But let me say this, that right of appeal is given because the wife is an equal partner. Even though her husband may have the last word, she certainly has the right to question that decision if things are not working out.

Let's say that Johnny makes a decision from left field to move to a new town. Helen then ask him about things like the school system, housing, the cost of living, and other very pertinent questions, but in spite of all, he feels strongly they should move. Let's say the family goes along with his leadership and things don't work out. After a time, Helen has the right to sit him down and make an honest appeal. Johnnie needs to listen well. Because you are the man you don't get to make crazy decisions and not be held accountable! However there is a way for Helen to make her appeal. See the Chapter "Who's In Charge?" The opening line of Psalm 23 can be seen as, ***"My husband is my shepherd . . ."*** Viewed in this light it automatically becomes apparent that there are two-character roles working within this principle: The shepherd and the sheep. The shepherd here is the husband and the role of a sheep is played by the wife. Please keep in mind that the sheep is actually the star of the production. It might help you ladies to remember that the shepherd is at his best function because of the sheep. We pick up our narrative at: ***"I shall not want."*** Putting that whole line of reasoning together we read it this way: *"My husband is my shepherd and because of him I shall never be <u>in want</u>"*. Let me add an editorial note here: When speaking of wants, it would be better to understand this as needs. Often people get this confused thinking that whatever I want should be supplied. Your husband/shepherd must take care of your needs and if he is able and wise often some of your wants.

The very heart of the 'Shepherding Principle' begins with the shepherd himself. Scripture teaches us that the shepherd is responsible for the welfare of the sheep, even to the laying down of his life for the sheep. This laying down of his life is not just in a time of crisis, or emergency, but rather it is a continual process of protection and provision, day in and day out. Scripture again tells us through Jesus' words that the shepherd is the door to the sheepfold. Historical tradition gives us a clear view of the meaning of this scenario. It was necessary to put the sheep in tents or makeshift shelters for protection from the elements, or perils of some kind. Interestingly enough, the tent or shelter was found to be without a door flap. The shepherd would place himself across the only opening. To get in or out one had to deal with a human door. Men are good at rising to the emergency occasion that calls for the protection of their wives and families, but this scripture actually implies a daily 24 hours, round the clock protection.

Before a man asks a woman to marry him, in principle, he had better settle it in his mind/heart that he is willing to become her door! The more modern term we use in some religious circles is that he becomes her covering. This all speaks to the responsibility of the shepherd, which is twofold. The husband must not only take the responsibility of seeing that decisions are made, but also, must take the responsibility for the consequences of that decision. Every woman must also make up in her mind, before she even considers marrying, that she will honor her husband as that door of protection.

Bill allowed his wife to enter into the labor market after she convinced him that their several small children were able to do without her constant care. Perhaps it was more due to her constant complaining and badgering than her convincing arguments which caused him to give in. He really didn't see it, but he was just plain tired of her mouth! Florence went back to work, first on a part time basis, which quickly developed into a full five-day week, with some overtime. Bill also noticed a gradual change in his wife's attitude. House, children, even Bill, all seemed to take a lesser place in her priorities. Bill sensed it almost from the beginning but was determined to say nothing. That decision cost him dearly.

Florence began to take up with some questionable women on her job. More and more during her off-hours from work, she wanted to be with them socially.

Bill warned her about the changes he was seeing so they argued a lot! *"My friends and I see things differently now. This is a new day. Women are more liberated,"* she argued. The consequence of Bill's decision, to let Florence return to work earlier, against his better judgment, cost him, and his four children their happiness. He did not step up and say, "NO"!

Before a woman agrees to become a wife, she must have it settled in her mind/heart that she is willing to allow this man to become her covering, her shepherd. This becomes more than a notion when the woman realizes that she must place herself under her husband's authority. I prefer to define it as her *Covering*. I'll try to clarify the difference in terminology here by making it clear that the husband is not her boss. She does not have to obey as though it is his way, or no way. Her *Covering* is like God expecting him to place a loving canopy of protection over her and the family. This Covering is motivated by the husband's love for her, and her total wellbeing. It can never be done out of his selfishness, or his need to be in charge.

You will find both Ephesians 5:22 and Colossians 3:18 saying, *"let the wife submit herself to her own husband."* Ephesians 5:24 further tightens the command by adding, *"So, let the wives be* (subject*) to their own husbands in everything".* A woman agreeing to become a wife should never arbitrarily make a major life decision independent of her husband. She should understand the risk of suffering consequences. If that man has been assigned by God as her *Covering* she cannot afford to disregard him at will. This has become so crucial a question in our day. Often, today wives are making more money than their husbands, or equal to him. The principle does not change at all. Nowhere in scripture is this ever implied. No matter how much you make your husband is there to be your covering, your head! Again, not boss, or in any way superior, just the *covering answerable to God*!

Sometimes, unwise women will develop their own pitiful sense of self-security. This usually happens after some tragic personal failure. These hurt women begin to spread their poison to other women willing to join in. Unfortunately, in spinning this web of darkness, it has the tendency of drawing in the unsuspecting. Some women with happy homes, and good husbands get sucked into these dens of divisiveness. Your husband may not be perfect, but regard him as God's gift to you. Be prayerful and thankful and God will bless you even more. On the other hand, the spirit of dissatisfaction will kill your deep-down joy. The Bible teaches us to rejoice and to learn to be satisfied. The spirit of discontentment and dissatisfaction will bring on disarrangement. When one gets into this spirit almost nothing will satisfy. Stress and depression will become your bedfellows for certain.

Florence rejected Bill's advice to break off her fast relationships with these new friends on her job. She felt that he was challenging her liberation. She saw nothing wrong with going out with these women. After all, they had their new hip life style really together. Bill, could not put it into pretty little neat words like Florence required, but he saw what it was doing to his wife. All he had to go on at that point was this feeling. This crazy feeling of his was not enough for her to make any changes in the direction she was traveling. These women were all about some fun.

Eventually, Flo started meeting her new companions in bars and other after hours places. Her home was no longer the place that brought her great satisfaction. In her earlier background she had been raised in the church, and seemed to delight in being involved in her local congregation. She now found church boring, and the people a bunch of religious snobs.

One night on the way home from work, she stopped at a familiar bar with Sally and Dee-Dee. While sitting there talking and sipping a coke and rum, three guys walked over. They suggested a ride in Buster's new convertible Cadillac. The girls began to dare each other and soon decided that they'd all go for a lark! The six of them headed out on a highway bound for some different kind of fun. Flo sat between Buster, at the wheel, and Stan. The other girls sat in the back seat with Bobbie. No one is quite sure just what happened as the sleek new car sped along Route 95. The police report was filed as a fatal head on collision with a bridge abutment!

I don't want to suggest that the consequences always end up in some physical tragedy, or death. Consequences vary both in type, and degree, as well as long and short range. We all wish that Florence was still around. Her refusal to let Bill be her covering cost everyone. She left not only a grieving husband and several motherless young children but look at the string of countless others that are left hurting because of her selfishness.

Ladies, before you say yes to marrying that man, think of all that your yes entails. You as an unmarried sheep, in this instance, unless it is an arranged marriage, have a choice of whether to accept this particular shepherd as your life covering, or not. Take your time! Natural sheep don't have your advantage to choose which shepherd they will follow. Now of course I am talking about a true shepherd who loves his sheep and will give up his life daily for the welfare of that sheep. A true shepherd does not abuse or neglect his sheep. He is subject also to consequences as well.

Spencer and Mamie have always had a problem. She chose too hastily. While visiting her aunt's farm one summer Spencer swept her off her feet and they were married by the end of that summer. Spencer wanted to leave farm country so they ended up in a highly industrialized city. Spencer's job didn't bring in as much money as they needed so she got an office job. Mamie was doing well until her husband showed up at her job and demanded that she leave right then. The office manager foolishly tried to step in and was promptly flattened by Spencer. *"A woman's place is in the home. That's how it is,"* he screamed at her as they disappeared down the hall and into the elevator.

Then there was the day that Spencer announced that Mamie could not go back to the little church that she had become greatly involved with. *"I want you home here with me on Sundays, and Wednesday night."* Mamie was crushed! She sought council with Rev. Goodfellow who sadly informed her that her husband actually had the authority to do what he was doing. His authority actually came from the word of God. Even though God would not agree with his crazy decisions. God gives to him the authority to make these bad decisions as the shepherd of their family. But boy oh boy, I would not like to be around when God starts paying off for his crazy foolishness.

Now I've heard critics differ with this by saying that no man can make another person sin against God. They are absolutely right. But, if that husband makes a decision, short of causing sin, he does have the authority over his wife. It is not a sin to be forced to become a non-church attendee. It is very stupid and shameful but really not a sin at lease on the part of the wife. It very well may be sinful on the part of the husband though. It is really sad if that ever happens. I would not like to stand one day in front of God and have to answer for that kind of craziness.

I think it is wisdom for a pastor and congregation to accept into membership a married woman, living with her husband, with his agreement. I don't like using the term permission. I think agreement is a little softer. It is great wisdom for the church to recognize that husband's headship. It may be a plus in winning that reluctant husband to Christ. This recognition of a husband's priesthood has worked for us more than once in our church. After all, the Bible makes him her priest whether or not he is part of the church scene or not. Now I would hasten to caution, that a man never make an idiotic decree to separate his wife and family from the church, just because he is the family head. Even if as head he may have the right to do so that would be like cutting off ones' nose from his own face. If you are not connected spiritually in a personal way your wife may be your best hope. With her chase or careful behavior there is a chance that you may be won to Christ!

The Word Itself in 1Peter3 is most powerful: *Wives, likewise, be submissive to your own husbands, that even if some do not obey the word, they, without a word, may be won by the conduct of their wives, ² when they observe your chaste conduct accompanied by fear. ³ Do not let your adornment be merely outward—arranging the hair, wearing gold, or putting on fine apparel—⁴ rather let it be the hidden person of the heart, with the incorruptible beauty of a gentle and quiet spirit, which is very precious in the sight of God. ⁵ For in this manner, in former times, the holy women who trusted in God also adorned themselves, being submissive to their own husbands, ⁶ as Sarah obeyed Abraham, calling him lord, whose daughters you are if you do good and are not afraid with any terror.*

Then a Word to Husbands*: 7 Husbands, likewise, dwell with them with understanding, <u>giving honor to the wife, as to the weaker vessel</u>, and as <u>being heirs together</u> of the grace of life, <u>that your prayers may not be hindered</u>.*

Even though the wife is placed under her husband's protective authority the husband is under the authority of Christ. If you hurt His sheep (Christ Himself being the Over-shepherd) He will not take it lightly. God will hold that husband directly responsible. Jesus speaks on several occasions about deliberately offending. Mark 9:42 says *"And whoever shall offend one of these little ones that believe in me, it is better for him that a millstone was hanged about his neck and he were cast into the sea."* Our man Spencer has never been free. He himself is a hostage. Eventually he allowed Mamie to return to church but it has not really helped his case. He has tried church himself but because he has never fully confessed and repented to God for *his sinful* actions, he goes about tormented and pitiful. It has affected every facet of his life, and will continue to do so until genuine repentance is made.

Once again, I caution the woman not to make the agreement to place herself under a man's authority until she is first of all, very sure of him, and and sure, of his relationship to the Lord Jesus Christ. Second, she should not make that agreement until she is very sure of herself and her willingness to submit in all things to this under-shepherd.

We need now to move on to more of the SHEPHERDING COV-ENANT. If you read down through Psalm twenty-three you should see that there is a seven-fold principle operating.

The husband as the head is expected to be:

1. *The provider of the wife*
2. *The leader/priest (initiator) of the wife]*
3. *The restorer of the wife*
4. *The protector of the wife*
5. *The comforter of the wife*
6. *The encourager of the wife*
7. *The healer of the wife*

I would like to sum up the role of the husband by generally calling him the Protector. This pictorial illustration might help us to visualize him better.

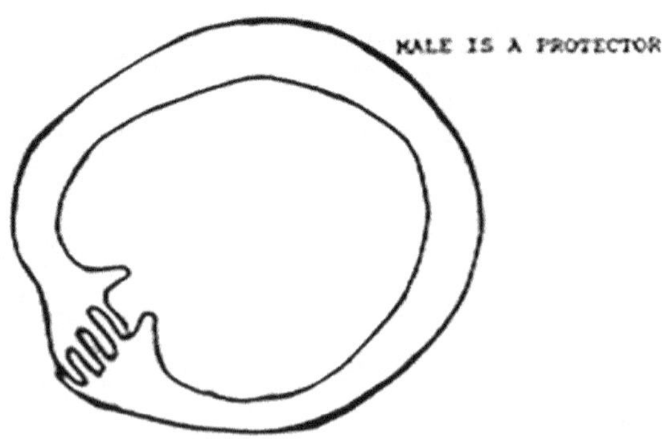

Figure A

I see him with his arms outspread in a wide circle like fashion. He encompasses all gathered inside his grasp. When the husband applies the principle of marital shepherding, it means far more than a willingness to give one's life in one final act of heroism. It is more like a commitment to being willing to die daily; a giving up, so that you may obtain. The husband must be willing to love his wife as an extension of his own body.

The wife is a responder/cradler and should expect to have her reasonable needs met through her shepherd/husband, and his:

1.   *Provisions for her*
2.   *Leadership/priesthood to her*
3.   *Restoration and renewing of her*
4.   *Protection of her*
5.   *Places of peace and comfort for her*
6.   *Constant encouragement to her*
7.   *Continual healing for her*

If the woman expects to have her needs met through any other channel, including herself, she is probably not ready for marriage. She should be aware that God has provided for her through her husband. If she rejects any of the seven principle factors to follow some other course, she is wrong and in line to miss a blessing. In an abstract drawing I picture a woman with her arms in a circle with hands folded inside as if hugging or cradling toward her breast.

Figure B

Reba wanted her husband to be her leader. Yet any time he would make a decision she would challenge it. She always dreamed of having a strong husband. I'm not sure, but she may have encouraged herself to grow up in a manner that called for a strong man to overpower her strength. She perhaps needed to feel especially conquered. Yet head games are not for married adults! Her husband tried for years to lead but felt the competition was too much for him. He finally dropped out and became a silent observer. Reba now complained more about his lack of interest in her, the house, the children, and everything in general. Even when she would back off for a while after reading a book, or attending a counseling session, it was not enough to entice him to venture into the lead role! They both knew that the role shift would not last long anyway. He was just plain tired, and frustrated. It is a sad fact that if a woman foolishly wrestles her husband out of his manhood role, there are too many women out there waiting for just half of a chance to show her how submission is done. These poor guys that seemed so dead and burned out, mysteriously come back to life, in the arms of these crafty women.

The man that is not respected by his wife is a man that lives in the shadow of destruction. The wife must actually reverence (deeply respect) her husband. To be respected in a loving way is a key need of the husband. There is something in the make-up of the man that flourishes when he is respected. This factor can cause that same man to be destroyed when disrespected. Many women, on the other hand, need to be constantly reassured that their husbands love them. This must be done verbally as well as through acts of kindness and affection. Some writers call this the act of cherishing. Actually, both of their needs seem to be different but in actuality are almost the same. ***A man needs respect,*** and ***a woman needs love***. They are pretty much the same, but find their differences in the vehicles of expression. Unless a prospective couple *plans to work on understanding how to supply these needs for a life time,* my suggestion is—***call off any marriage plans*** until the commitment can be *made for a lifetime.* You see the commitment goes beyond just surface level love. It has to be a commitment to continuously do that which produces love. You cannot effectively do what you have no knowledge or understanding of.

The marital covenant is the underlying basis for strong marriages. It is the stuff that fuels successful dreams. It should be a firm agreement up front. After learning, understanding, and accepting the responsibility of being the shepherd of the wife, the husband must make that total commitment to her, and to God. His prayer might be in part:

> *"Oh God, make me an instrument of thy protective peace. Let me be the covering of my wife, that she for life never has to look out-side of our relationship for strength.*
>
> *May she find in me comforting leadership through the exercise of my priesthood. Let me bring to her healing restoration, and renewal. This let me do in praise of Thee O' God. Amen.*

After learning, understanding, and accepting the role of the precious Sheep towards the husband/shepherd, the wife's prayer might well be:

> *"Oh God make me an instrument of thy responding peace. Let me be grateful and accepting of my husband's spiritual, physical, and mental covering for life. May I ever look to You through his loyal priesthood. Let me receive his constant healing that I, through him, might be renewed in Thee. May I find favor with my husband as a token of praise to You O' God. Amen.*

Men and women both need love but they often need it differently!
Women usually need a type of secure love that touches on their
emotions and their need for security and reassurance. While on
the other hand men look for respect, which tends to comfort them
and send a strong message of self-respect to their love zone.

Figure C

It is far better for a couple to begin learning this principle b*efore* they attempt to say, "I do". These perspective mates can study each other without the pressure of actually being under fire. Before marriage they have the luxury of examining themselves to see if they are ready for this kind of lifetime commitment. It should trouble a man who can't honestly say to the woman he's about to marry, *"I intend to be your shepherd providing for you for life".* Yet *if he cannot say it, and mean it,* he had *better withdraw his proposal.* On the other hand, *the woman who cannot honestly say "I intend as your wife to live under your loving protection in obedience to you,"* just *better call it off!* Paul addresses the Ephesians Church (5:28), *"So ought men to love their wives as their own bodies. He that loves his wife, loves himself."* Earlier, 5:22) he instructed, *"Wives, submit yourselves unto your own husbands, as unto the Lord."* He prefaced both of these statements in verse 21 with ten simple, Precious words, *"Submitting yourselves one to* *another in the fear Of God". If this is too much of a commitment for either to make up front then they should not go any further with marriage plans.*

On the other hand, let's speak for a moment to those that are already married. Perhaps you did not know this shepherding principle before you married. Let me say as strongly as I can; you cannot walk away from each other because you didn't know what you were doing. If you begin now to apply this SHEPHERDING PRINCIPLE the wheels of possible disharmony will begin to reverse themselves. It is never too late to start over the right way.

I wish I could share this principle with so many of the Hollywood stars that face a break up before they even get started. So many have messed up their lives in meaningless marriages. It is so sad when the Tiger Woods family, Eva Longoria and her Husband Tony Parker, and everyone's favorite Sandra Bullock and her bad boy husband Jesse James, all took the hard road to divorce. The interesting thing is that in all of these situations, and in most of the other ones coming out of this town, infidelity is implied. No one ever explained to them I guess, that the shepherd and his sheep are responsible to each other for life. With this kind of shaky commitment, no wonder the results. Bed-hoping actually tears away the ones flesh element of the Triangular Plan. Once again, I liken it to painting a collage using paper, paint, and glue. Like I described in the previous chapter this method unites all of the elements into a constant pictorial blend that cannot be separated. To try and go back and pull these things apart is to do irreparable damage to the composition. Yet I am a believer of hope. If these couples would go back and allow God to begin putting in the repairs it is quite possible that some of these marital tragedies could be salvaged. I have seen it happen in the lives of ordinary people; why not stars? Again, ***"It is never too late to start over the right way"!***

I want to share now a letter written to a spouse who was in just this kind of trouble. This person confessed that they were feeling no love for their spouse of many up and down years. They just wanted out!

They felt that since there was no love felt at all it was alright to think about getting a divorce. It might surprise you, there is no scripture that I'm aware of that says you may divorce because of a lack of love. That's man-made stuff not God's desire. Along with the name I eliminated all references to gender both to protect the persons involved, and to show the contents of this letter to be of universal in application, and value.

(Dear Spouse:)

This is a follow-up to our counseling session. There is so much that I want to share with you about learning to love your spouse properly. You see I do not agree with those who feel that love comes naturally. In fact, I believe that like anything else of value, it must be worked for, and on!

God has created us to be a marvelous and intricate instrument of thought, and action. The thought control center is both able to produce thoughts that motivate action as well as justify actions that follow thoughtlessness.

True love springs from our mind, not our actions. Our actions result because of what is in our mind. The thought initiates in the center of our mind then expresses itself as our will. This will is transmitted to other departments of our being that begin to express themselves in accordance with our will. To help you love, we must work on two levels at the same time.

First, you must realize that God wants you to love your mate! To operate as though you made a mistake in marrying is to defeat yourself—and God's plan. So, first be assured that God wants you to love your mate. It is His Will! *Let that thought initiate in the very center of your mind permeating your total self.*

Secondly, realize that if it is God's will, it too must become your will! *This is the only way you can be obedient to God's will. The strongest facet of love out of 5 Greek terms* *for love is called Agape. (Each of the 5 is needed to make the whole.) Agape is determined and unselfish. It says, "I will love you-because I will to love you." You can see that the only determination comes from you. It is not based at all on what your partner does, or does not do. It is unselfish because it refuses to look at what you get in return. You love because you want to love him or her for their own good!*

By now you might be saying, "But Pastor that's too hard for me to do when I have no desire to do it." I agree with that but there is one tremendous way to accomplish this. Since it all began with God's will for you to do so—you simply go back to God for the needed power. You begin praying to God to increase your will to be in line with His will. Ask God to pour into you a deep love never before known to you for your mate.

Pray daily—all throughout the day. Read over, and over, and meditate on 1 Corinthians Chapter 13. Let the Lord begin filling your mind with the entire deep wonderful, passionate thoughts of loving your mate deeply.

See that person as that wonderful strong, protective, and sensitive one so able to meet every need you have. Let your mind be free to day-dream about this new love who's hidden treasures you increasingly long to investigate, and have completely engulf, and consume you! You want to be enveloped by it, as well as it being able to envelop your spouse in your newfound desire to love. May God increase your love and allow you to find new areas of depth in Him.

Love,

Your Pastor,

CHAPTER 2

DIFFERENT STROKES

Genesis 1:26-27

*And God said, "let us make man in our image, after our like-
ness: and let them have dominion . . . over all the earth. So, God
created He (them); male and female created He them.*

I ALWAYS DELIGHT in doing pre-marriage counseling. Often, I begin
one particular session by exclaiming to the two young hopefuls, *"I have
discovered that men and women are different"*! Right at this point I always
pause to watch the expressions of my two eager charges. Their faces
usually go from enthusiasm, to bewilderment, to disbelief. How could
they have chosen a naive counselor that had just made this age-old
discovery? I then continue with a chuckle, *"Oh I've known for a while now
that there are a lot of physical differences. I don't mean the bumps and lumps,
but actually our whole orientation is different."* "Men are not like women and

women are not like men.' Now that I have you in bewilderment too, let's examine what I've said:

A LOOK AT THE PROCESS

If we return to Genesis, I think we can discover some interesting truths. In some places God talks about man the human being. In other passages, He talks about man the male, or in Genesis 1:27, man the female. In Genesis 1:26 when God speaks with his triune self, *"Let us make man in our own image"*, I know that it is hard for some guys to accept, but God is not talking about the male alone being created in the image of God. He is talking rather, about the creation of **mankind** being created in the image of God! For certain, there is a common human bond in males and females, who were both created in the Image of God.

Genesis chapter 1 gives us a summary view of the creation process, while not attempting to go into any great detail. We get more specific details in chapters 2 and 3 of Genesis.

Look now at chapter 2 verse 7. Here I believe we see a clear reference to man the male and the specific creation process.

> *2:7 And the Lord God formed man of the dust of the ground, and breathed into his nostrils the breath of life; and man became a living soul.*

After years of studying the entire text, I believe the proper interpretation to be, *"and man (the male) became (the first) living soul"*. We know that man the male was created first, then the woman-the female, came second. There are several jokes about that part of the process. One speaker told his audience that the reason God created the male first was that; *"God didn't want to have any advice"*. Now while you men are laughing about that, hear what his wife who was in the audience rose to say, *"Well, we all know"*, she said, *"That anytime you are going to make something great, you always make a rough copy first."* The audience went wild with laughter, but, there was no come back on that. So, whatever in the mind of God caused Him to create man the male first and then, man the female second, that's how God planned it period! Let's look further at Gen. 2:18 for more convincing evidence:

> *And the Lord God said, "It is not good that man (the male) should be alone; I will make him (the male) a help . . ."*

It isn't until verses 21&23 that God begins to create the woman. The humorous muse about a rough copy and a finished copy, might provide some validity in another way. Understand, there is a clear difference described in the creative formula here. I used to wonder just why these two varying descriptions existed. I now believe that this was not just, *'writer's style'*. God was sending a clear and precise message. It is true the actual details of the process are only there in outline form. Yet, even in that there are two different and distinct outlines. Verse seven of chapter 2 says that the man was formed of dust from the ground. God then breathed the breath of life into the man's nostrils. It does not attempt to specify what kind of dust because that kind of knowledge is not even needed. Next, we are told that what God formed needed to go through a second step: **God breathed into the nostrils the *"Breath of life"*.** Then at this point what was formed begins living. Then verse eighteen sheds an all-important insight: Even though man the male had been formed by God, and literally breathed into living existence, he was still incomplete.

I find that it is so interesting that God created the earth, separated the waters, spoke light into existence, and saw that all of it was good (Gen.1: 1-24). God created seas then initiated a system of how grass, herbs, and trees would grow, and reproduce and saw that it was all good. God then created two great lights, called the sun and the moon, and gave to them their functions as rulers of the day and the night, added to them stars, and saw that it was all good. God then turned again to the waters causing it to abundantly bring forth moving creatures, and whales and flying fowl in the firmament of heaven, and God saw again that everything was up to specifications. He saw that it was good! He blessed them saying, *"Be fruitful and multiply."* And after God said, *"Let the earth bring forth (every) living creature reproducing (after its own kind) (following its own species) cattle (after cattle) creeping things (after creeping things) everything according to this (everlasting) system:* And God saw that it was good! "Good-good-good." Six times we see this in chapter one, and then one additional very good at the end of the chapter.

I find it extremely interesting that the statement of approval and endorsement was strangely missing after God created Adam the first actual man. There was no party thrown; no celebration in verse seven at all! It was like God just went on with His work, no big deal here. He created grass, herbs, and trees and then gave a hearty endorsement, but when it came to his finest creation, the only one, made after His own image, there seems to be silence. Why is that? Well, *I believe that it is not really silence, but rather a big pause!*

Remember after he was created, Adam was given an assignment to administrate over various functions, like naming the animals, etc. This he did apparently with commendable service. Why the pause? I feel that the pause was very necessary for Adam. He needed the special experience of working, and planning by himself. I can imagine Adam trying to bury himself in his work, not unlike what men do today. But it didn't quite fit. I'm sure he probably tried carrying on some meaningful conversation with his animal charges, to no avail! There was something missing! Something was incomplete in his life, and he now knew it through personal experience! Personal experience is a great teacher, if we get it right!

I assure you, the woman that God created and presented to him was not an afterthought in the mind of God. The timing was vital. Had they both been created simultaneously the experience would have been different. Adam would not have experienced the great painful truth of actually needing to share his life with another human being. Because he was on the scene first, I'm sure that he took on a kind of protective role. He was the one who filled Eve in on the way things operated around there. If we think of it, there is probably little purpose for the animals to have names other than to relate information to other human beings. God didn't care what Adam named them, and the animals could care less what they were called. There was no two-way conversation between man and animal. The only reason that names are given, or are used, would be for communication and identification!

So, we maintain that even though the man and the woman were not simultaneously created, their creation was paired. One was created to need the other. The male was alone and in need of companionship, sensitivity, and compatibility. The female needed protection, leadership, and appreciation. The male was made from the raw materials of the earth. Nothing refined or strained, just 100% natural fiber. The female is made from those same materials, (now a bit refined) but the source is different. She was fashioned out of material (pinched) from the male that was taken directly from the ground. It was the same material but a different creative coming together. Same product-different process! Different in process but both united by **God's *"Breath of Life"*.**

Adam from creation it seems had a missing factor built in. That factor was that he would be incomplete without his female counterpart. When God refers to Adam being *"lonely"*, an interesting question comes up. Was Adam lonely because God made him and then realized that His creation could not find companionship? Or did God design Adam with a complete plan in place? In other words, was there a designed flaw in the fabric? Yes, I believe that the latter is true. God already knew that Adam would be lonely because it was already programmed in. Adam thought that he was complete. He went around Eden doing his little thing. Can't you see him talking to the animals and thinking that was all there is? It never says in the Word that he ever complained about being-lonely, or having something missing in his life. Personally, I don't think that he ever did. I don't think that he was even aware of his need until God brought Eve to him. He couldn't know that there was a perfect way to fulfill that void in his life. But boy did he catch on when he saw her for the first time!! You've got to see the excitement pouring out of his heart when shouts out at the sight of her, *"She is bone of my bones flesh of my flesh!"*

Isn't it interesting that the first time God said, *"It is not good,"* was in connection with His first image bearer Adam? Stay with me here, God was not displeased with Adam His first creation. God was just stating that He was not finished yet. There was more to come in this unfolding divine drama.

And the Lord God said, (Gen. 2:18) *"It is not good that the male should be alone. I will make him a help, meet for him."* One of the most misunderstood-misquoted passages in the scriptures just went by us. How often have you heard people use the words **"help", a**nd **"meet"**, not as single words in a sentence, but as a term? I've heard preachers, pastors, and even marriage counselors use it as a term "Help-meet" or "Helpmeet". In these contemporary times there are those who have tried to update the term by saying, "Help-mate". Friends, there is no such term, biblically speaking! To use *Helpmeet* in any form is to be totally uninformed; and to use *"help-mate"* is to further compound ignorance.

God said flatly, *"I will make him (Adam) a help . . .* That's it, there is no more! A help! The next word meet, is not the second word of a two-word term. *Meet,* here and in just about every other passage, means *suitable, fitted, or fitting for.* No other term or title was ever implied, or intended. Even to use the term "helper", is to do violence to what God said. The woman was not created to be a second-class helper: that is like calling in a hired gun to help shoulder the responsibilities. No, God was not creating a helper, rather He brought to Adam (Gen. 2:22) his completed self. Adam recognized her right off as, *"Bone of my bones, and flesh of my flesh."* Even the original terminology *ish* and *isha*, man and woman, indicates that we are not talking about a man and his helper. The creation process is significant. One commentator ventured, *"Eve was not taken from the head of Adam so that she could be created to be over him. Nor was she taken from a bone in the foot to be under him, but rather God took her from Adam's side so that she could walk beside him."* Adam's completeness was found in Eve as an equal companion. Likewise, the woman was completed in her husband. For either to be a helper was to lessen the importance of either role. They are equal in position and in ranking.

In studying the first two chapters of Genesis, we can conclude that God deliberately pointed out how differently He formed man and woman. I think that this difference in process helps to illustrate several things. First, it illustrates unity. If the man was fashioned from the dust of the ground, and the woman sculpted from the rib of that same man, are we not dealing with the same creation material? Secondly, if the sameness of materials illustrates unity, then the differences in the creation process must illustrate diversity.

Funny, today there is a big push for sameness when actually God went to considerable effort to promote diversity. His human creations were just as much unalike as they were alike. If He really wanted them to be exact clones, the creation process would have probably been identical, and maybe even simultaneous. Yet in Genesis, He spells out in enough detail for us to get the picture that something is at work. The man is created from the dust of the earth that God built. The woman is created from the rib of the man that was created from the dust of the ground that God built. And still later, come the children from the womb of the woman who was created from the rib that was taken from the man, that was created from the dust of the ground that God built. One dust job, one rib job, and a later birth job. Diversity at work! All the time using the same material.

If God then points out diversity, you can be sure it is for a good reason. And more than likely a blessing is also intended. In order to prevent keeping you in suspense, here are my thoughts on why the intended differences.

DIFFERENT MINDS

One of the greatest blessings that men and women have going for them is, that they are not of the same mind. Or at least usually they don't arrive at the same mind from the same direction. It's like the husband walks down Main Street to the corner where he meets his wife who has just come up Center Street. Each coming from a different direction, but both headed for the same destination. There they now stand at the corner of Main and Center Streets, having had two different arrival experiences. They may now take these diverse experiences and blend them into one useful expression. Major decisions should be made together. Because we are different it is likely that we will use a different set of criteria for final judgment. Our perspective is likely to spring from entirely different sources, even if our aim is the same.

Here's a personal example: My wife and I discovered that it is difficult for us to clean a messy room together at the same time! We have two very different philosophies. Dot's method and approach is to dump all the clutter in the room into the middle of the room and begin organizing. Somehow my computers over-load, and burn out at that point. My method is to begin with one small corner of the room, clean it, and fan out from there until all is done.; two very different approaches to the same problem. I get really frustrated when I come in and see everything piled in what looks like a war zone. It usually takes her all day, and at days' end when there is no time and energy left, the remainder of the pile ends up in some corner until the task can be finished. Now on the other hand my "clean as you go", method frustrates my wife. You see by days' end I have not been anymore able to complete the task either. An equal amount of clutter and an equal amount of order seem to emerge from both methods. We have had to come to the conclusion that neither method is wrong, and neither method is perfect. We can work together at separate times in our own little special ways. Wasting time arguing the virtues of the methods won't get the job done. If Dot works her little, "From the center of the pile "magic, and I do from "Corner to corner", we are helping to attack the common problem—*mess*!

IN ORDER TO BLESS

Married couples who feel that they must see eye to eye, with no differing opinions are missing the intended blessing. God has created us with different minds, stimulated by different stimuli. If we would take the best of the two worlds, and use that best, just think how strong a decision for a plan of action, it would be. Yet the great wrestling match for one-sided domination rages on.

Gordon dominated his wife. He decided everything for their marriage. How she dressed, what she cooked, where she shopped, how they behaved themselves in public, everything. The woman was literally a little clone of her husband. The fact is, Mary did have an excellent mind. She chose to play second fiddle to her husband. She was quite capable, but never seemed to challenge any of her husband's decisions, at least not publicly. Theirs' seemed oddly enough, to be a happy marriage. My only thought was, *"I wonder how much better this marriage could have been with a joint sharing of ideas and opinions"?*

Marriage is oneness made up of two people. If you take the best that these two individuals have to offer, allowing it to mix and blend the result should be strong and positive. It's when we continue to try in opposite ways, without even a brief moment of understanding and cooperation, that what was intended by God to be a great blessing, becomes a great conflict.

Charlotte complained that she did not need her husband Ronald to keep acting like her father. *"He tries to shelter me too much,"* she grunted. *"He does not like for me to visit my girlfriends in the Bottom, because that part of the city has a rough reputation."* She goes on to fuss about his concerns about certain of her friends. She feels that because she is grown she should be able to choose her friends without his interference.

THE EMOTIONAL MALE

What Charlotte failed to realize was that Ronald, by nature, tends to be a protector. That's the natural role of the male. It is true that a man's body is usually larger and his muscles stronger. These physical traits are pretty well established. Yet as we research the Bible, we see man the male emerging as a protector. Males are territorial in their scope. We are prone to mark out a territory, set boundaries, and erect walls to protect those boundaries. We are likely to look out and see something coming close to our walls. Our usual reaction is to plant ourselves outside of those walls to warn and challenge those wandering too close. Our honor and sense of self-worth is often tied up in our struggle to maintain our territorial rights, and our families. Our failure to protect can be internally viewed as personal defeat to us. Sometimes men allow a personal defeat to become a matter of our honor. It is hard for us to separate honor from duty. Men seem to be wired that way. It just comes up without a lot of provocation.

Once as a young boy I was attacked by an older youth from the neighborhood who ran up and grabbed me from behind. He held me in a semi-chokehold with one arm and stuck a lit cigarette to the side of my temple. I yelled and struggled free. My next move was toward home. I walked there quickly holding my hurting face, not ready to challenge, or defend at that time. The boy for some strange reason followed behind, taunting and insulting me. It was not until I reached home that the full impact hit me! I started in the house when suddenly a new direction overwhelmed me. This idiot who had already burned me, harassed me, insulted me, was now standing in front of my very door challenging my territory. Immediately, I went into action by grabbing one of the glass milk bottles that was stored behind the front door for the next days' pickup and delivery. I rushed forward to the top step planted my feet like a quarterback and prepared, arm stretched backward, to deliver a glass bomb that would have done Donovan McNabb proud. Fortunately for that kid, my mother hearing the commotion came out and plucked that milk bottle from my hand, just as I reached the firing point of my arch. Relieved of my weapon I don't think I missed a beat as I sprung forward, and downward to meet my challenger in the middle of the street. There we went at it until separated.

What happened that turned a scared crying boy with no fight in him, into a raging gladiator ready to destroy? Suddenly territory became a factor. Honor was on the line! When the incident began, there were no real concerned witnesses around. Later, a crowd had gathered. I could not afford to let my territory go defenseless. My home turf and my fans were now a big part of my cause for action. Looking back, I kind of feel sorry for that guy. Somebody should have schooled him to never bring a fight to the home grounds of an opponent. I was not going to let my people down! I wonder how he would spin this story, smile?

The scriptures indicate that all men have a basic need to be honored, or respected. A wife who disrespects her husband has the potential to emotionally destroy her husband. Honestly, there is a built-in need. A man functions on respect. See Ephesians 5:33, and I Peter 3:6 for this interesting difference in men. Proverbs 31:23 paints him as one who sits in the gate of the city. The gate was like a town court where all of the important things of life were discussed. It for these men was life's forum. When a man sat there, he wanted (*actually needed*) to be respected. The woman of Proverbs 31 knew the importance of her husband looking good in the eyes of the other men (*in that special Men's space called the 'Gate'*).

I put on an old shirt that needed ironing one-time to go and do something outside of my home. My wife stopped me dead in my tracks. She would not let me leave in that condition. "*You represent me*", she exclaimed! I got the picture really quickly. She was not going to allow the possibility of some woman entertaining the thought that Dorothy was not taking care of her man.

We've got to admire Sarah. Abraham involved her in a disparate move because he was afraid for his own life. He asked her to say that she was his single sister. He felt that her beauty was so great that he would be killed if it were known that he was her husband. His charade could have led to adultery. Sarah had every right to call him a cowardly dog, and worse, but I. Peter 3:6 says that she actually called him *"lord"*. Women's libbers would probably call her dumb for not leaving him. I doubt that she was in anyway dumb. You see she knew that she could crush Abraham because of this serious blunder. Yet the Bible says that she reverenced her husband, or in other words, she held him up in an honored position. Even though he was wrong, she did not hold him up to public ridicule. Now privately, we don't know what Sarah said to old honest Abe. But, whatever she said, if she said something, (I believe she took care of business behind closed doors, as most women that I know would) she still managed to respect her husband outwardly!

I knew a guy who went off track and began to play around on his wife all over town. Several of her friends tried to get to her to tell her what was going on. Each time they would try to begin she would cut them off abruptly. Soon all of her friends felt sorry for poor Joanna, *". . . because she doesn't know what that husband of hers is doing"*. What was interesting to me was that on the outside Joanna never seemed to change. She did not bad-mouth her husband, or allow anyone else to do so. Was she a fool? I think not. Several years later I met her husband and marveled to myself how domesticated he had become. Our meeting was brief, but I saw no trace of the arrogance and brashness that had once been a part of his character. Obviously, Mama Joanna took care of business - *but behind closed doors*! A repentant man who makes a mistake, but feels that he is still genuinely honored, and respected, is more likely to want to recoil and try again, than one who feels like the phrase, *"From dust thou art, to dust thou shalt return,"* was written for him!

A woman is naturally a cradler. She presses her family inwardly to her breast. The male will often fight for his family and sometimes others because of his honor, his territory, his dignity, etc., but the female's motivation is usually somewhat different. She will fight to protect her offspring, her mate, or even her territory because she feels it her natural duty to protect them for *their* sake. Her honor is rarely at stake. She sacrifices for her family because it does not occur to her that there is anything else to do.

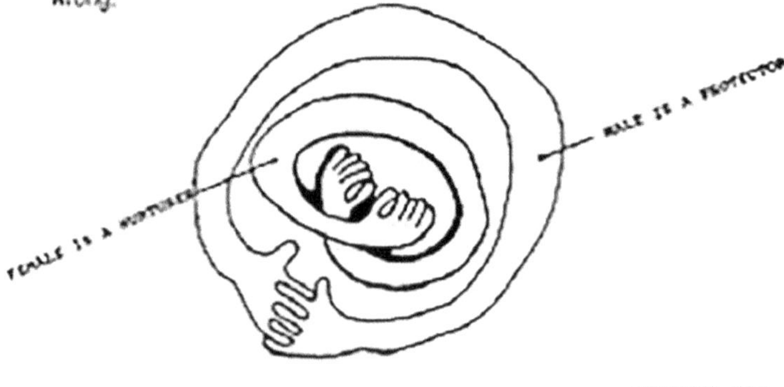

Figure D

Women have been known to give the last of the food to their young in hopes of their survival. The man in some cases might feel that if he can eat the last morsel that he would have enough strength to find food to feed his family. Let the reader understand that these illustrations are only broad generalizations and not intended to label, or set in concrete specific actions or reactions.

Because a woman is normally a cradler, she seems also to be more sensitive to the affairs of the heart. Thinking about gender difference, I have a notion that many men may be just as sensitive, but for reasons may have been taught, or trained to filter out much of the emotional elements. Considered how we raise our boys with tough toys that promote no feeling? How can you evoke a genuine feeling of love from a Tonka Truck, or a Spaulding football? As a result, our little boys grow up to become men that show more compassion racing converted 4x4s, down a mud track than they show love-starved wives. They become better at spending time watching sports for hours, than listening for five minutes to a wife pour out her aching heart throbs. If a man needs respect to survive, a woman has her own special survival needs. A woman needs to love and be loved!

A husband will probably find that he must assure his wife on two fronts at the same time. He must first assure her as her Provider/Protector. *She just naturally expects him to go out and slay the dragon for her.* She may even introduce into their relationship little test dragons of his faithfulness and love. Changing light bulbs, moving some kind of furniture, adding gas to her car, are not always tasks that could not be accomplished by the average woman. They may however (without his knowledge) be presented as tests of the man's devotion to her.

There is a second assurance: A lot of men are fooled by the old expression that, *"A woman marries for security"*. Security yes, but not only security in the physical sense of provisions and protection. *She also needs his verbal reassurance that he loves her.* She needs to hear almost daily these simple words, *"I love you"*. Hear them not just as three simple words like you would say, *"Good morning"*, at the office, but *"I love you"*, with all of the passion and depth that comes from way down deep inside of you. It's like the words from the song Maria. (from West Side Story) *"... Say it loud, and it's like music playing, say it soft and it's almost like praying ..."*

My Pastor, the late Rev. Allen Mack, used to say humorously, *"Add a little something special to your 'I love you', like 'Darling', or 'baby', or 'sugar'.*

Also adding a couple of those special titles together never hurt, like 'Baby -dar-ling', 'Sugar-dear', or 'Honey-sweet'." However you say it, **husbands, say it. Say it, say it, say it!** Mean it from the depths of your heart, and don't wait around until it's time to make intimate love to remember to say it! Your wife needs to hear it throughout the day.

To be considered a good husband, remember two things are needed and required by most women under the security clause:

1. Provide and protect her physically and emotionally.
2. Provide and assure her verbally, with emotional words of genuine compassion and love.

The ultimate design is for both the man, and the woman to realize who they are, what they are to do, and how they are to do it, and to be willing to give their all in a team effort.

Differences should not be a curse! In fact, these differences were *designed by God to be used as blessings.* Maximize and blend what the two of you have. It will add strength to the relationship.

CHAPTER 3

BUT YOU ARE SO DIFFERENT

BASED ON THE heels of the previous chapter, we would like to borrow this next chapter pretty much in its' entirety from one of my previous books, **Marriage: The Rules of the Game.** We covered some very important elements in that book that bare repeating here. Of course, we've added some new content where helpful.

A good part of the struggle in marriage is that we are so different! He may see it one-way and to his amazement she has a completely different view. She may want to do something that she feels is important, and to her consternation, he is very reluctant. Why can't they come to agreement about what each of them sees as just plain simple?

Jan wanted a well-designed home. She loved to ponder House Beautiful and Better Homes and Gardens magazines. HGTV seemed to never go off in their home.

She dreamed of having a comfortable show place that was well planned. Ernest just wanted a comfortable place to call home. He was content to have an old easy chair in the corner of the living room where he could read the daily newspaper while glancing periodically over the top at the old vintage TV. Nothing in their home had changed in 15 or 20 years, with the exception of cable, which was a mothers' day gift from one of the kids. Same chairs, same TV, same carpet, same flower centerpiece on the same coffee table, all of it the same. Jan wanted for all of those years to make changes but her husband controlled the finances and would not budge. Their children grew up and left home and still they could not make one change. Jan became so burdened as the years rolled on. She felt under appreciated, unloved, and unfulfilled. She had been a stay-at- home-mom for all of the years they had been married.

She decided one day that she was not going to go out like this. Jan went out and found a job that was well suited to her skills and talents. She never made it to college but through the years, she had continued to study floor plans and design concepts in every library book and magazine, she could get her hands on. She went for an interview one day and was hired on the spot at a home- decorating firm that specialized in home makeovers. Her personal pleasures and a deep sense of accomplishment at first were vicariously experienced from the satisfaction of other homeowners. Their praises electrified her. Then one-day Jan with, plans in hand, brought her crew to 1645 Elm Drive. They ripped, tore, and smashed everything that was in the way of a new look. Ernest was out of town on a job assignment. A week later he put his key in the door and was shocked and bewildered. His key had obviously admitted him into someone else's home. There was nothing familiar to him. He backed out of the door and spun around to look at his mailbox. Yes, this was his address.

He couldn't believe his eyes. What in the world had gotten into his wife? This must have cost a fortune. Jan didn't care about the money; it was now time for her dream.

Mavis and Frank decided not to argue over their house decorating differences. Mavis had a tremendous eye for design. Frank decided that the best thing for them was to take his hands off so that she could be free. He admitted that he didn't even have a clue, but he enjoyed her work and the praises that other people lavished on Mavis. He realized that it was more beneficial to appreciate and go along with the program than stand in its way. His support pleased Mavis and she always tried to please Frank.

Yes, by gender we are often different in how we view things and how we respond to things. Yes, and even how we express those things. Researchers say that on any given day a female will use 15,000 words during that day. On that same day a male may averages about 9000 words.

Differences do not have to separate partners. In fact, God intended for there to be differences. If two spouses agree to meet at the northeast corner of Broad and Main Streets at 12 noon on Monday, it is not always important the route that is taken to get there. Suppose the husband likes to drive along Broad Street as he comes from Center City. He likes to see people scurrying around interacting with other people. People to people is a turn on for him. On the other hand, his wife prefers to drive to their rendezvous by using Main Street. She needs to unwind from her busy schedule. Part of Main Street winds around through the City Park and eventually along a river. While driving along she gets to appreciate nature's dramatic production. The factors that are important in this illustration are time and location. The agreed time of their business is 12 noon. The agreed location is the northeast corner of Broad and Main Streets.

So often, couples engage in some serious arguments over how to get to a point and miss the important stuff that makes up the essentials. If we decide to save for a car because we need basic transportation, the car color and the interior fabric is not all that important. Several years ago, I needed to buy a new truck. I have always wanted a classy red truck. I almost dreamed red truck. In fact my plans were to have my old truck painted red. But when I took my truck for service, a Service Representative convinced me that to put more money into a 16-year-old truck and to continue to put the kind of wear and mileage on it for what I was using it for, was not using wisdom. My journey home was not a very pleasant one as I thought about the insults to my old standby. He managed to shatter my dream with a dose of reality. How could he say those things about my trusty friend? I went home content to stay the course. I told my wife about the visit and she said, *"Well we certainly need to pray about it,"* and pray we did! Surprisingly, after praying about it, the next day I went to pick out my shiny new truck. On the way I rehearsed to my wife all of the vital features I wanted, since it seemed like I was compelled to go this way. The truth is, I loved my old truck but if I had to change then I was going to get exactly what I wanted this time, starting with the color. Approximately half of an hour later I sat behind the wheel test driving a sparkling new Nissan truck. It had most everything that I had on my list. I could do without the automatic door locks and cruise control. The only big thing missing that was on my list is that the truck was silver not red. They didn't have a red truck in stock. They did give me the option that they could possibly locate what I wanted in the area but that it would take another day or so. And of course, there would be an extra service charge for the pickup and delivery. Add to that, it wasn't even the color red that I wanted. Bottom-line I had already delayed my trip by a day to get this now much-needed vehicle. My options were to forget this deal and rely on my 16- year-old road weary friend or delay further in hopes of finding the great red one (*not the color red that I really wanted*), or be satisfied with a pretty silver one. Incidentally, the reality is that wherever I drive everyone loves my pretty silver truck!

The reason I shared a part of my personal life with the reader is to illustrate the process. Red was indeed important to me but the need for comfortable, reliable transportation was a larger consideration. Add to that the tight time factors. It was not that I didn't like the silver color I just preferred red. When it comes down to it, our differences should not weigh too heavily in the bottom-line decisions. Preference certainly is important, but a compromise might be helpful in getting you to your bottom-line. If we spend precious time feuding about style, color, process, etc. we may be setting ourselves on a collision course that will blur the arrival point.

When there are decisions to be made you must take time out to discover what the bottom-line issues are. What is the purpose of the thing, to be considered? What does it involve? What is the desired outcome? How will it benefit both or all? Will it impact each person differently? If there are disagreements, what are the possible compromises? How best can we implement and proceed with the plan that is going to help us? Becoming angry leading to arguments and confusion is probably going to take you farther away from a workable solution. Stay cool and pray your way into the best solution.

Doris wanted a new house. This had been her dream since college graduation. Her husband Steve agreed that they had a need because the new baby was due in about six months. While driving home from work one day she saw a new housing development being built. She got off at the next exit and doubled back to see it up close. The sample house was still open so she went in. It looked marvelous inside! She could hardly wait to tell Steve. When he joined her the next day he had some serious doubts. *"Baby this housing development is smack between two highway Interstates. The truck traffic at night will be deafening. Besides I've been wanting a house that is close to my job. I think the inner city is the way to go." "But I want a new house,"* Doris offered, *"and it's in our price range."* For two months they went back and forth on this house vs. the inner city. One night the topic came up when they were having dinner with some older friends. Madeleine said, *"Your apartment is too small with the baby coming, but how long will it take before living there becomes impossible? Certainly, it is not until the baby begins to become more active. So that gives you more time, right?"* Then Tony weighed in; *"Is the need really that the house be a new house, or a good house? One that fulfills all the basic needs you will have to raise your family? Isn't that what you are really looking for?"*

Doris and Steve began to look at their dilemma differently after that conversation with the Wrights. What they needed was to concentrate on the real needs; new was not one of them, nor was being located in the inner city more than just an attempt to cut down on travel time. Not too long after that they discovered a beautiful modest house in a quiet little village. It was less than half an hour away from both of their jobs. Once they started praying about their real needs, God began to open a door.

Now we do recognize and understand that background as well as gender can be factors in how we view situations. If we refuse to be open to some give-and-take on an issue, it could likely cause the one party who feels most deprived of ownership to feel forced into acceptance. In some cases, it has caused one party to feel forced into a radical departure from the process. This is when some partners bail out and go into seclusion. They actually refuse to be engaged any more. They become pensive and silent. That's when we get the *"Anything you say,"* treatment, or *"Whatever you want,"* We know in tone that is not what that person really wants. This is not agreement. This is a part of the great bail out! Sometimes some issues are allowed to become very personal in nature, when really, they should be viewed strictly from a non-personal vantage point.

Sometimes when our differences get in the way we just need to sit down and talk. Begin to say honestly how each of you feels about this object of discussion. It is usually helpful when **party B** repeats what they feel **party A** is saying about the topic. If there are corrections or additions **party A** should then clarify. Next **party A** gets to state what they feel that **party B** is saying with that same commitment to fairness, and again, with a non-judgmental view. Most issues can be worked out if **both parties** *feel a sense of ownership.* Compromise should include the best of both worlds when possible. Cedric's college major was history. He lived and breathed history for about 10 years before he married Brenda. The local library thought that it was a great idea to invite Cedric to head up a research project. The project would highlight the library's founders and their great contributions over the past 75 years. Because Cedric was married to Brenda who was a Fine Arts major and local painter, the committee later thought that it would be a real touch of class to have them collaborate on the project. In this instance it was not a good idea. They were as different in their ideas as they could be. Instead of them working together, they scrapped about everything. And I do mean everything. There were areas that would have worked well, but once they set out on a hot collision course, they could not even see where the strong points were. It really should have been Cedric's project. He was the historian. Brenda could have enhanced his ideas with her art background, but Brenda wanted it to be her project, done in her style. She saw what she could see, but failed to try to see what Cedric saw. The results of their finished efforts looked pretty good on the outside but certainly could have been more outstanding. Because of their failure to genuinely collaborate and seize the moment, what could have been outstanding, had to settle for just good! Just think of the stress that resulted. Both came away with a reluctance to ever collaborate again. This was a sad state of affairs for a couple that stood at an altar and pledged a lifetime partnership.

A selfish spirit breeds selfishness. A spirit that strives for unity will likely attract unity. Does it really matter whose idea it was in the first place? If a couple enters into the project, plan, program, or event and work hard together does it really matter who swings the hammer or who brought the nails? I remember talking to a couple somewhere who I think had completed a project in their home. The project was probably very nice but they kept picking it apart to tell me what each of them had done. Frankly I could not have cared less who did what. I just wanted to enjoy the finished piece. How they got to the northeast corner of Broad and Main Streets was of little consequence to me.

Husbands and wives are usually different in their approach to a challenge. That's all right if they can maximize their efforts together in the journey. Recently, I was listening to the car radio when I heard Bishop Gilbert Coleman, a local Philadelphia minister, say, *"The beauty of the house is in its harmony, and the security of the house is in its loyalty."*

Harmony and loyalty certainly work for a strong marriage. Yet harmony does not mean that everything is the same. Rather, it suggests that there are different, even contrasting elements involved in a combination that makes for balance. Remember the Stevie Wonder song, '**Ebony and Ivory**' speaking of the black and white keys of the piano working together to make perfect harmony?

Considering the kind of balance that makes for harmony, we suggest that it may not be always a symmetrical or 50/50 system that works. It is possible to balance a 15-pound weight with five pounds on the other side of the lever. It all depends on where the fulcrum is. We call that kind of balance *"asymmetry"*. Personally, as an artist I find that I love symmetrical groupings of things. I also love asymmetrical groupings as much as I do symmetrical grouping. But by self-analysis I have discovered that I really can't stand when groupings are so random that they fall into neither category. When there's absolutely no balance there is no harmony. Couples should look for ways to blend. Compromising, blending, and assessing by both contributors make for harmony. Hey married folks try to make your differences work for you! This is the blending of both worlds. Likely, it is the intention of God for you.

While reviewing this chapter with my friends Dr. and Mrs. Jean Wilkinson, Dr. Jean offered what I felt was a classic illustration. He talked about the time when he and his wife were planning to hang some paintings in their home. They agreed that what they wanted was for all of the paintings to be hung at eye level. Several days later when he came from work he discovered that his wife Zuline had begun the project on her day off. She was proud of her accomplishments but her smile quickly faded when she saw the bewilderment on Jean's face. They had agreed on eye-level placement, but as it turned out she was 5'6 inches tall and he was well over 6 feet tall. He actually had to bend down to appreciate the paintings that she hung.

They could have had a major disagreement over six inches. What they found was the need to find a distance somewhere in the middle that was comfortable for both of them. All problems or conflicts cannot be solved that easily, but there has to be some middle ground. If both partners are being reasonable they will seek a middle ground! To strike a compromise that seeks to bring satisfaction to both spouses should always be the goal. I should love to please my spouse. It is not robbery to do so. My spouse's aim should be to please me. Together our attempts at harmony make compromise desirable. My happiness unselfishly feels good when I know my spouse feels good. ***Remember, eye-level is relative. Don't take it personally!***

CHAPTER 4

YOUR WIFE WANTS YOU TO KNOW

Sometimes husbands are simply baffled when it comes to understanding their wives. The problem often stems from the husband trying to figure it out from his own male perspective. Here's a news flash: Men and women are different! "Wow", you say, "How did you come to that astounding conclusion"? Well, I am not trying to tease you with that statement, just trying to confirm what you've always felt.

Rev. Jeannette Flynn, the former Director of Kingdom Ministries of The Church of God, shares this little personal history. When she was getting married, her husband Chuck wanted to show his love for her so much that he could hardly wait to give her a special wedding gift. She began to open the pretty box as he stood looking on anxiously. Once she got into the big box her once gleeful spirit melted. What she discovered in the box was not some beautiful, personal, gift, but instead, a cooking pot. To Chuck this practical gift would make his new bride so happy. It was understandably difficult for Jeannette to hide her disappointment. She knew that he wanted to do something wonderful for her. Just at that time in life he didn't have a clue. She told me that they still laugh about that.

The great reality is that we are wired differently causing us often to be very different in how we think about things, or how we react to them. Sometimes even with the same stimuli, because of that intricate male/female wiring system, we may see differently, triggering different reactions.

Husbands learn pretty quickly that the things that stimulate them sexually are probably not exactly the same things that motivate their wives. It is pretty commonly known that most men are highly stimulated by what they see. Some experts have guessed at an 85% rate of response through the eye gate for men. This is one of the major reasons why the pornography industry has taken off at such an alarming rate. Guys like to see it in their heads. Of course, this is not good because generally it is not their wives that they are viewing but some substitute body, which is bound to take them off of the real mark. The Bible has a remedy when it tells us to, *"Enjoy the wife of our youth,"* Proverbs 5:18, and then in Ecclesiastes 9:9 it says, *"Enjoy life with the woman whom you love all the days of your fleeting life . . ."* and Prov. 5:15 *"Drink water from your own cistern* (faucet) *and running water from your own well.*

I believe these passages of scripture are pointing to the same triggering mechanism that causes the disconnection. Returning to the wife of our youth is a very strong urging from God, to return our minds to the original beauty that captivated us in the first place. God knew that part of the human makeup was curiosity. The mind has the ability to wonder, then wander, without discipline. These passages along with Malachi 2:14, instruct us to set our inner eye on a fixed target. That target is your wife's body as it was in its' prime. It is a clear call back to that moment in time, when you desired her the most.

Curiosity will tantalize and intrigue us into imaginary adventures. Once these forbidden adventures occur, they paint indelible photographic pictures on the walls of the mind. These pictures unfortunately form a type of permanent file that can come open at almost any time. These visual/ mental files tend to force us to make comparisons with what we should not have seen. The more you see, the more opportunities there are for these comparisons to float to the surface. If we are to overcome this dreadful state we must be lead back out of the same door that provided us entry. It must be the willful turning, and convincing of the personal mind.

Comparing your wife to some electronic image is totally unfair to her. She was made by God and given to you for your enjoyment and satisfaction for a lifetime. Actually, she was uniquely designed for you. Also, it should be said that you were designed for her.

I don't think that I've ever talked to a Christian man who did not admit that he knew that pornography was wrong and against God's plan for his life! The problem is that most who have fallen into this abyss were led captive through their curiosity. Curiosity is like holding onto a string that never allows you to reach its' end on its' own.

The antidote for this behavior, beside genuine prayer, is complex but in the mix a change of mind/heart and a raw determination to exclude all others must be there. What you have is what you have. Appreciate what you have. Set your affections on those things that are at your hand. Be satisfied with what God has given you.

It is likely that your wife will never be able to perform in some of the positions that you have seen in cyberspace or in video trysts. Please know that what you have probably seen is staged. It's just drama! These folks make money by exciting their viewers. It does not have to be real, just exciting. More than likely in their private sexual lives they are not performing as they do on camera. I wish that I did not have to tell you to think about it, but for the sake of argument, some of these things presented are just plain dumb and would lack any level of real-life comfort. Remember, the industry is growing on unrealistic fantasy. The love of money is the root of all evil.

John wanted his wife Susan to dress up and pour stuff on him, etc. Where did he get this from? He got the idea from something he saw. Susan tried to comply with some of the stuff he requested but most of it was just plain ridiculous. It was novel in a sense, but ended up so uncomfortable that neither of them enjoyed the moment. It was a total waste of time plus the extra clean-up. John's insistence that they follow this route made his wife feel that she was not good at meeting his needs. Struggling with all the other things that married people struggle with, she could now add a measure of lowered self-esteem to her list.

Your wife does not want to be compared with some image that you saw somewhere and now is stuck in your overdrive. She probably has her own struggles with her weight and how she looks. She does not need you to come along and try to mold her into a hooker wannabe. She wants you to know that it is hard for her to satisfy herself in her own view. If she has given birth it is likely that there are bulges and patches of unwanted fat that she tries to deal with; and often dealing not too well either! If she is beginning to age, even the slightest bit, she is waging constant warfare on body spread, and wrinkles, and gray hairs and on and on. The very last thing she needs is for the man in her life to show dissatisfaction with the very thing she is already battling. She needs your support not your condemnation.

Larry's eyes followed and dwelled too long on every shapely young woman that passed him. It was not even that he was appreciating the passing woman's appearance but his gaze seemed to indicate that his thoughts were going much further and deeper than appropriate. Jenny felt that each time it happened it was a direct rebuke of her, and the more than 35 pounds she had gained after having their two children. She tried hard using several popular diets but the weight kept on coming. Because of his implied rejections of her, she ate to medicate. Inside she was still the wonderful woman he married. Larry's carelessness is very crucial. It affects the next steps toward if, and how, Jenny recovers her self-esteem. Actually, Jenny should know that Larry's roving eye has nothing to do with her weight. Larry has to deal with some internal character issues.

Wives are generally stimulated more by acts of kindness and tenderness! In our second book, **MARRIAGE: The Rules of The Game**, we make a real point about the acts of kindness and tenderness, coupled with supporting deeds. In fact, I believe it is so powerful please allow me to quote extensively from chapter 6.

Generally speaking, kind words, tender touches, and supporting deeds stimulate most wives while most husbands are turned on visually. The great mistake that many husbands make is in thinking that since we are turned on visually that our wives are stimulated in the same manner. The sight of fancy lingerie is more of a guy turn-on thing than it is for women. Certainly most women like receiving gifts and the look of pretty things, and perhaps even the thrill of light filmy garments touching them, but remember, the turn-on is a male thing. Her sexual stimulation comes from a far different source. Men can rise to the occasion quickly through the eye gate. We can become aroused at the drop of a hat. We could be compared to a racecar going from zero to 60 in a matter of a few seconds. Our wives are not like racecars but more like the old 'T model', and 'A model cars' that were patiently hand-cranked to turn the engines over. Then after cranking the engines had to sit idling until they were warmed up.

Almost every magazine these days features some headlined article on how to stimulate super erotic moments. "101 Ways To Turn Your Woman On"; "The Hidden Treasures of Intimacy"; "Fifty Ways of Love Making"; "Finding Her Secret Spot" . . . on and on they go. Listen, you can pretty much save your money if you remember "WTD". Kind words, tender touches, and supporting deeds. This is shared because it is seen pretty much as a need that most women have. It is not shared to maneuver or manipulate. It just makes all the sense in the *world that if it is a need that can be supplied easily by husbands, that we learn to build it into our regular routine. This is the formula that can make **you**, Mr. Husband, into Mr. Great Husband! Remember, **"WTD", kind words, tender touches, and supporting deeds.***

The words should be kind words of recognition and appreciation not words of ridicule and condemnation. Loving caring words that help her know that you value her greatly; words that identify her as the one closest to your heart.

What I can remember about the TV character Archie Bunker is that he almost never had any intentional, endearing words for his wife Edith. He ridiculed and put her down at every opportunity. The show's writers projected her even in the face of all the putdowns as a dutiful, jovial glutton for the punishment her husband gave. Remember now that was TV; it does not work in real-life. Trust me, Edith Bunker does not live in your house!

Positive communication in a loving environment is enhancing. I try to remember to always say thank you to my wife for cooking all of the great dinners she prepares. She goes all-out not only in the preparation but in the presentation as well. She decorates my plate the way a master chef would. She sees to it that the table is always set with a place-mat, etc. She loves it when I notice these things and say, "thank you." When we eat out, she always thanks me for dinner. Our love is regularly expressed with kind words, and loving deeds of appreciation.

A husband who learns and practices the art of soft words turns away wrath. Now when I say this, I am in no way suggesting or condoning dishonesty and subterfuge. What I am encouraging is that husbands should find the easiest and nicest way of communicating your heart. Then remember, don't let all of your conversations center around business, the bills, the kids, the house etc. Tell her the nice things about herself. Let her know how much you appreciate her; the sacrifices that she makes for you and the family. These are the things that most husbands receive and accept, but rarely really notice. If you begin to notice them it will put you in a different league altogether. The ultimate home run is when you make her feel good about herself. I haven't met too many women who are not concerned about their appearance. "Am I getting too heavy"? "Do you think I've lost too much weight"? "Is my hair getting too long . . . too gray . . . too dull", etc.? "What do you think about the way I dress lately"? The questions that wives ask about themselves never end. If the husband begins to volunteer compliments before the questions come, he will meet a deep need. When he begins to address her need for verbal reassurance, her appreciation level for him will increase.

I remember learning in the schoolyard that little poem/motto that went, "Sticks and stones will break my bones, but words will never hurt me"! Now that little slogan helped get me through Elementary, Junior High and Senior High School, but beyond the school context, when you think of it the slogan is pretty dumb. Words can hurt! They may not have the ability to break bones but they certainly have the potential to break hearts. I think I even knew that back in kindergarten while being called some pretty awful names. The poem just helped to launch a counterattack so that the little perpetrator wouldn't know that you suffered a hit. Yes, words can certainly hurt. That's why we caution couples to use the most positive words they can use in conveying a message.

The good news is that words can heal! I remember running to my mama after one of those schoolyard bullies sent a verbal brick through my poetic fence. But mama, before she did anything else, would sit me down and begin pouring on the verbal oil. She would remind me how special I was and that no one who really knew me could ever say something like that about me. Well, when I walked out of a private head session like that with Dr. Mom, I was ready to go back out on the battlefields of life. Her words healed me!

They not only healed me for that occurrence but put healing in me for a lifetime! Husbands must be ever so careful to put healing into their wives. The secret is to place in them words that affirm them and benefit them before they experience an outside hit. Confidence builds walls that protect.

Wives who feel protected and appreciated are far more likely to feel intimately aroused. Romancing her early in the day may set the kind of thrilling tone for her that escalates and expands through the day. Whether or not the marriage act is experienced that particular night is not of the greatest importance. Romance can be cumulative. It just may accumulate over a couple of days stirring up great sexual passions that explode into great moments for each of you.

(The above quotations are from my second book **MARRIAGE: The Rules of The Game)**

Again, we make the point that wives are generally stimulated more by acts of kindness and tenderness, coupled with supporting deeds.

Helen and John had been married for about seventeen years. They had three children, a nice home in the suburbs, and the normal debts that married people have. John started to notice that Helen had become very restless and dissatisfied about almost everything over the last several years. He tried to figure out where all of this negative stuff was coming from. Trying to fix the problem, he decided to pour money into their house and whatever else he thought he could do to satisfy her unrest.

One good thing that marriage counseling provides is a format to help people talk more freely. Married folks should make a time to talk to each other on a regular basis. But so often when something happens to block that freedom, it gets increasingly easier to build walls that separate. The next thing that usually happens after the wall starts building is a tendency to justify why there is a wall.

After several sessions it was discovered that what Helen really wanted was for John to show more personal interest in her, not their house and other things. *"Take me out of here. Let me have a real life!"*, she screamed at him one day. Finally, she was able to confess that she was feeling trapped. For most of the seventeen years she was having children and keeping house. There was more to her than just that!

In her mind, John got to go out into the world and see things. To her, John's life was an ever-changing kaleidoscope of events. To her, life was centered around children, and house work. Trying to financially struggle to maintain the suburban dream limited their time and money to do other things. She felt that John never really took her out just to show her off. She felt that socially she had become a misfit. Maybe she had always been a misfit she began reasoning. She resented being defined solely on her mothering and domestic skills. She wanted John to love her for something else. She was intelligent, and gifted, but lately it seemed to her that all validity was based on the kids and home. It did not help her when even her church celebrated her as one of its' top moms of the year. Was she only a good mom? Was that the sum total of her existence?

What John could not see, was that she needed to be appreciated for her personhood, aside from the things she did. To base everything on her serving skills alone was shallow in her eyes. Yes, she really was a good mom, and a good wife who kept a good home, but that was what she did, not who she was! Her current dissatisfaction was a cry for help.

What John could do to begin reversing some of her malaise is to begin simply looking at the things that she was complaining about. Use these things as road maps toward a different future. Rather than try to defend the things that irritated her, begin to highlight the things where she was seeking recognition. She wanted to be recognized as the beautiful woman in his life. She was discouraged about the few pounds that she had gained after giving birth to their three children. She was still a beautiful lady. Their comfortable home had become, for her, a private prison. John needed to celebrate her apart from their home. He had to begin taking her out to places where she could be noticed. In order to do this, he had to recognize that a wardrobe change was necessary. The clothes that she wore to PTA functions and even church services probably would not fit the bill.

Once he really got it, he began to reinforce his appreciation for her as a person. Instead of buying her toasters he started buying her dresses and shoes, and lots of personal things.

Helen needed his time. She began to enjoy sharing her thoughts about life and the ways of the world. He discovered that she loved to write poetry and had actually been doing it and tucking it away in all kinds of storage places. John began helping her to gather these gems of creative genius and fashioning them into book form. He found her a publisher and they launched an unexpected career. Once he got it, he really got it! He helped to unleash a wonderful secret side of his Helen.

CHAPTER 5

HUSBANDS AND THEIR SECRETS

IT IS OFTEN said that women are difficult to understand. This is mostly said because women tend to change before their first pattern becomes what we thought was going to be a pattern. Confusing? Well yes, you've got the point. Just when you think that you have figured it out there is likely to be another wrinkle in the fabric. The good news for women is that this little confusing trait actually seems to draw men in like a moth to a flame. The mysterious ways of a woman both frustrates and delights us. I talked to a young husband whose wife is expecting. He was both frustrated and intrigued with his wife's crying. *"When I ask her what is wrong she can't tell me." "Sometimes she is crying because she is sad, and sometimes because she is happy; but there is never a real good reason for either."* I just smiled and reassured him that everything would work out fine. I thought of Pastor Paul Earl Sheppard's recommendation that we all become Panologists in our philosophical dealings. According to Pastor Paul, *'Panology,'* simply says that it will all pan out in the end! I told the young man to be patient and kind and as helpful as he could. Perhaps some of what he was experiencing was due to the pregnancy but it was not too far off from some of her regular behavior. I didn't want to tell him to stay tuned, because after the baby arrives would come a whole different set of emotions from his wife.

Now after having said all of that, let's realize that on the other hand, men have their own degree of difficulties. It is true that men tend to be a little more predictable in their behavior, but this does not at all explain the behavior. Honestly, we certainly can do some weird things too. For starters let's look at some of the toys and games men play with.

Dirt Bikes, Play Station, paint ball, Grand Theft Auto the list goes on, but I think you get the idea. Many of these toys and games are centered around aggressive behavior. Men tend to like things that blow up and self destruct. Don't overlook the growing fad of home theater rooms, and 'Man Caves'. Men are buying huge TVs and media screens with surround sound to do nothing more than to get the action up closer and louder to us. If it is going to blow up we want it so up close and personal that it makes us flinch and duck for cover. Violence is not only tolerated it is expected. My wife and I have discovered recently that we cannot watch some types of movies together. I have no answer when she wants to know how I can stand to watch all those car chases and bullets flying. There is something really weird going on when you see the mildest of men watching violent movies and TV shows.

Another strange question is: what brings on mid-life crisis for some men? These men can go on through life without causing anyone to raise an eyebrow, and then suddenly change overnight.

Ronald was doing pretty well in life. He had a wonderful wife and loving daughter. He was moving up the corporate ladder and the money was really good. Suddenly, he wanted to be a ladies' man. He picked up some willing woman and went through some kind of sexual escapade. Tiring of this first affair he started another, and then another. We lost count after that. He was finally discovered when his wife's friend Janice spotted him checking into a rather seedy motel. Thinking of himself to be than he was, he lost absolutely everything.

Certainly, all incidents of mid-life crisis do not go into, or lead to affairs. The behavior can take many paths. Some men suddenly get interested in dangerous adventures, or sports that previously were not even anywhere on the radar. Why would 50-year-old Rodney, out of the blue, decide that he needed to become a race car driver?

Our thoughts and observations lead us to believe that a mid-life crisis in a male, signals some kind of personal unrest with ones' self. It probably causes a man to do an evaluation that concludes that he has not done very much with his life up to the present time. It pushes on his mind that he needs to do something before it is too late. So, then may come a plunge that seems to come from nowhere. He may feel that he is running out of time and needs to do it now. It is an inner crisis that might just be based on no facts at all, or on some inner longing to be heard, or seen, or anything. It may be, and usually is, all in the mind of the person. Others around may be completely satisfied with what that man is, or what he is doing. I think that it is very related to that same lifelong drive that causes a man to need to be respected as a sign of love and approval.

More male weirdness can be noted when we see that the male brain can cause men to be turned on sexually, for no apparent reason. A piece of paper thrown across the room might end up producing a sexual thought. Even though you know that you, dear lady, are not turned on that way, don't forget that your husband is likely to be coming from a whole other direction sexually. You both must find a way to see to, and fulfill each other's legitimate sexual needs.

You know another area of strange behavior is that men tend to be very territorial. We read about men who fatally fight over a parking space. Years ago, in the Philadelphia area, two brothers in law, who happened to share the same house, got into an almost fatal fight during a democratic primary, because one was a Hillary Clinton supporter, and the other a Barack Obama supporter. What were they thinking? Perhaps they were trying to lessen the vote by one? Yes, men do have some difficult issues to define manhood.

Maybe when men accuse women of being difficult to understand it is because our own big bag of difficulties is just very different from theirs. We kind of mentally miss each other because we are concentrating on different things. It can be like two trains passing each other in the night, going in opposite directions. Both on tracks right next to each other, and just as determined to reach the next station.

Sometimes it appears on the surface that we don't share the same emotions. Generally, it is thought that men don't cry. I'm not sure that is true of all men. I believe that all men at some point in life do some crying. What may be different about our wives, and to our undoing, is that much of our crying may be done on the inside. We tend to keep everything on the inside and this is not the healthiest thing to do. Women usually express how they feel on the inside. They are not ashamed to let their inner emotions out in the open.

In most of my early manhood years I don't recall crying much; especially with visible tears. However, I have noticed that as I've gotten older the tears flow much more easily. I now cry while watching touching movie scenes, and such things that play on the strings of my emotions.

When Senator Barack Obama was elected to be the 44th president of our country I was away at a conference in Phoenix, AZ. That night, I was in my hotel room watching the world-wide celebration and I shed tears of joy; especially watching Rev. Jesse Jackson openly weeping on TV. Two days later at the end of the conference, I listened to a friend, Rev. Suzanne Haley address the large gathering of ministers and I really openly wept.

Suzanne spoke of her disappointment at not feeling like she could freely celebrate a great moment in history because the day before while the world was celebrating the historical victory we in our National conference were silent. The great historical event was not even mentioned publicly by our leadership. We knew the reason was, no one wanted to offend those that voted for the other candidate. However, Suzanne's challenge brought relief. That day I did not even try to wipe away the hot tears flowing down my cheeks. My soul needed some cleansing! It was a time to cry.

Men on the surface may be warm and friendly, but that is usually as deep as it gets. You will need an extra special pass to see beyond the surface. After a while it becomes almost a natural thing to deal on the surface of things. We were either taught, or learned in some way that it is *"manly"* to deal on the surface and hide our deeper feelings.

It is always interesting to me that women can go to the ladies' room and strike up a conversation with a complete stranger. It is not likely for men to do that. Generally speaking, men don't hold conversations in the men's room. Occasionally, they may exchange a brief greeting grunt, but rarely does it go any further than that. In fact, too much men's room conversation probably would raise a caution flag. It is somehow thought not to be very manly.

Taking it a level beyond Rest room conversation most men are very good at covering their emotions. Perhaps it is a learned response, or maybe a bad experience, that has taught us that showing any inner feelings is somehow going to detract from our manhood. So, we become experts at dealing on surface levels.

So, my dear sisters, please note this: Part of a man's wrapping is to cover up his inner privacy. He is not likely to be open about all the things he is feeling, or thinking. It may in time come out in dribs and drabs, if you are patient. Again, generally, men are not very comfortable when they are badgered about the things hidden in their heart/minds. Notice that when men are troubled or cornered they become almost monosyllabic. On the other hand a sister may blurt out the whole thing while a brother will cut down to fewer words than usual. Don't mistake his lack of words as a sign that he is without thoughts. In fact, when men are silent it very well may signal that their thoughts are actually running deep. Remember there are usually layers involved. Think of it the way onions are constructed. Each layer down goes closer to the heart.

The secret to getting to a man's heart is listening carefully to the few words that he is offering. Accept these few words and pray for him. The likelihood of him telling you more is tied up in how you accept his limited early offerings. If you try to probe and pry it will likely push him the other way.

Men tend to be very egocentric. Because of this egocentrism they often link their manhood with situations and events. It may help a woman to understand this male ego trait if we compare it to how she feels about the acts and events that make her feel loved. Interestingly, this is the same way a man feels about his need to feel respected. Women need to feel loved like men need to feel respected. Love and respect are pretty much the same emotion, colored by gender. I like to refer to Proverbs 31:23 when making this point. Notice the reference to this wonderful woman taking special care to make sure her husband looked good in the gate. The background of this is that the city gate was like our modern-day City Hall. It was there in the gate that all business was taken care of. I am pretty sure that marriages were arranged there; along with divorces and any other official things. This is probably where the major debates and lawsuits took place. This was the place where public policy was set. Scriptural theology was handled here as well as mandating just how it was to be applied in the home. This lady was concerned about her husband's appearance in this special place, and made sure that he looked good! We have a modern expression that may work here: *"Clothes that make the man"*. Perhaps a little shallow but does demonstrate a certain *esprit de corps*. She expressed her love by making him look good while he expressed his love by representing her well.

Hebrew/ Asiatic culture, which probably provided the back drop for the writing of Proverbs, allowed only the men of the city to officially gather in the gate. It probably provides an early look at what we now refer to as *"A good old boys club"*. Only the men of the town were invited.

It seems that what women were facing biblically was a *"Stained glass ceiling"*. In today's world, I'm sure that this practice would not stand very long. Although, extremely partial to men, scripture does mention a woman named Deborah as a judge in Israel. Perhaps there might have been other women leaders, but I think that you get the point; it was thought to be a man's world. Unfortunately, this has carried over in some of our circles today.

Returning to the why factor in the statement about how her husband looked in the gate, is very telling to how most men view their public persona. Most men like to be seen, and seen in a certain way. Even when I dress down I want to achieve a certain signature appearance. I think it says volumes about me. Yet it is not saying that I only want to be seen wearing casual clothes, because when I want to dress up, I am interested in making a signature statement as well. I admit that I am complex, and I guess it only tells you who I am at that particular time. Having said all of that I'm not sure that men now in general are vastly different about wanting to be seen.

Topping the factor of men wanting to be seen, is men wanting to be heard. Now I know that we have talked a lot about the silent male. Many men could have the motto, *"The fewer the words the better"*. However, this does not mean that they don't want to be heard. Not wanting to talk is different from not wanting to be heard. This is perhaps the factor that seems to derail some wives. The Proverbs 31 woman understood that her husband had to look a certain way in the gate in case he wanted to speak but by all means he needed to be heard. I have a good friend who happens to be a bishop. When entering a room full of clergy, a certain amount of attention and respect is accorded to him. It is not just because he is a bishop. His wisdom over the years has brought this kind of honor and respect. He really does not have to say a word. His presence speaks volumes. Should he decide to speak he definitely is heard by all in attendance.

Proverbs 17:28 says *". . . and he that shuts his lips is esteemed a man of understanding."* Some have said that it is better to say nothing and be well thought of than to speak out of turn. One old adage put it this way, *"It is better to be thought foolish, than to open your mouth and confirm all suspicion"*. If you want to honor your husband listen to him, what he says, and does not say! Listen to his heart. Respect what he says and he will talk to you more. Badger him and he will likely retreat. Let his few words have great weight. Respect is not just a desire on his part, but it is needed. If you disrespect a man enough he can feel defeat and failure. This is true especially if he perceives disrespect coming from someone on the inside. Wives occupy the first position in the man's heart, and then come the children. You must work hard at training the children in how to respect their father. You can also help him to posture himself to get their respect. Some men just don't get it. These guys could use a little help from you, but be gentle! Take care in guarding their most vulnerable place, a potential injured ego.

Inside of most men abides a champion—a slay-a-dragon spirit. Men want to conquer something and bring it back on their shoulders. This is part of a man's nature. Take that part of him away and you will see a man beginning to feel useless with feelings of failure looming near. Too much of these heavy feelings weighing him down and you can be sure that a state of depression will emerge. Men who are suffering can make unwise decisions and sometimes stupid choices.

Bennett was a smart guy who never felt quite comfortable with his wife's political career. She was not an actual office holder but was recognized all over the country for her political connections and her abilities to influence law makers. Bennett accompanied her on many of her speaking engagements. People would jockey for an opportunity to be in her presence on these occasions. Bennett would be somewhere twiddling his thumbs in a corner cringing, while trying to look important. The green-eyed monster was waging strong warfare on him and Bennett was losing.

In his wife's eyes he was appreciated for his companionship and what seemed to be support. April did not require him to be, or do anything spectacular. She loved him just the way he was. They never talked about her career choices. She thought that everything was all good. But Bennett could never get over how he appeared to himself. *"I'm just the 'Go for' around here"*, he would often joke.

Many men in a similar situation have gone on to adjust, or found a way of addressing the issues with their out-front wives, and worked out some kind of understanding, or even a compromise. Unfortunately, he did not. He began pursuing the interest of other women who did not have a rock star status. Eventually he allowed himself to drift into infidelity. These women were eager to massage his fragile ego. The devil set him up big time. He lost the love of his beautiful wife, his relationship with his teenage daughter, and on top of everything else, he contacted HIV Aids.

Let me quickly add, April was not at fault for the marital break down. Bennett allowed himself to be intimidated by her success. He should have seen it as their joint accomplishment. After all they were supposed to be one. Perhaps she should have seen some of the hidden divides in their relationship, but she didn't. He was not forthcoming at all. She loved him and really did value him, but he could not see himself as a worthy champion. What he told himself became louder than her words of appreciation. Scripture warns us that what a man thinks in his heart actually sets the stage for his own reality!

What your husband thinks about himself is important to his personal health. This encompasses mental, emotional, spiritual, and yes even his physical health as well. Many times, you, my lady, can hold the key. Remember, that big guy with the voice deeper than yours, may be carrying around with him a less than strong ego. Archie Bunker may have picked on Edith because he was intimidated by her good qualities. What an interesting thought.

By now I have a few wives upset because of all of this emphasis on the man. Why is he so special, and what about the needs of the wife being heard? Well, the name of this chapter is: 'Husbands and Their

Secrets'. I tried my best to represent you in the previous chapter. This is not about wives right now. Trust me, I'm trying to help you—not hurt you. I'm trying to help you get into your husband's heart. Just think about Aretha Franklin's song RESPECT. This will get you through that illusive door and into his heart. This is where you need to be. This is where he needs you most. Even if on the outside he has not realized it. Once you gain entry you are in a prime position to hear his heart. Again though, gentle is the way. Never malign or ridicule him for his thoughts. Listen and support. Once he senses your love and genuine support, he will safely confide in you.

CHAPTER 6

READY, SET, GO! WHAT'S THE PLAN?

Philippians 4:7&8

And the peace of God, which passes all under-standing, shall keep your hearts and minds through Christ Jesus.

Finally brethren, whatever things are true whatever things are honest, whatever things are just, whatever things are pure, whatever things are of good report . . . think on these things. (Remember this illustration from Chapter 2?)

TWO FARMERS WITH little else to do one day began arguing over who was the best shot. After endless argument, they decided to go out to the barnyard to prove it. The first farmer found several discarded tin cans and placed the cans carefully along the top rail of the wooden fence. He then strode back to the porch where he picked up his rifle and took careful aim. Ten times he fired, each time sending a can sputtering and spinning into the air. The second farmer smiled with confidence as he found some other cans and placed them on the fence. He returned to the porch and lifted his shotgun to his shoulder. *'Blaaamm'*! the gun kicked in response to the farmer's squeeze on the trigger. The ear-splitting blast sent both cans and fence flying.

There was no doubt that the first farmer was a good shot. All ten cans were hit by single bullets. Ten shots; all hits no misses. He established his purpose, set up his target, took aim, and fired. How well he did can be measured simply. He would either hit, or miss. We automatically can know whether he is a good shot or not.

There is indeed a problem with the second gentleman's claims to marksmanship. How do we measure it? Did he have a purpose, yes? Did he set a target, yes? How true was his aim? The purpose was there, and the target was in place, but there just is no good way to measure the results in relationship to the stated purpose. We are not sure that after taking aim the old farmer hit, cans and fence, or blew the fence from under the cans. His stated purpose was to demonstrate his marksmanship. He chose a weapon that could not have helped validate his claim, relative to the target.

A wise couple will immediately begin firming up their goals following their trip to the wedding altar. Aiming blindly through life is not a good practice. I suppose that anytime a couple sits down to plan, and to set goals, is good. Better late than never, but best is in the very beginning of the marriage journey.

If you have been following the progression of this book, you will notice that almost from the beginning I have insisted on the couple engaging in meaningful communication and planning. The kind of planning that an unmarried couple does is not the same as the planning they must do after they marry. The early planning done during the engagement period is meaningful as a base of understanding, but now they must sit and hammer out the final goals and methods of working.

Don't get so busy that you fail this all-important process. Catch up is hard, and the longer it goes the harder it becomes!

Tammy and Earl in chapter 1 had no joint plan. Tammy had her own plan which included having a family-owned business. On the other hand, Earl just wanted to have a regular job, making regular money, living a regular life, being a regular guy. He did want a very fancy sports car, and all the household toys that men like to play with but that's about as close to a goal as he came. He didn't even try to develop much of a plan to get these toys. He just assumed that his wife would work, pay the majority of the bills, and have extra money for him when he wanted it. His money was his own. He never ever let his wife know what his salary was. This may sound a little bizarre but I've found that that is not an uncommon complaint. I have heard many women complain over the years that their husbands failed when it came to supporting the family financially. They claimed that their roles as working mother, and helper, became also 'main breadwinner'. With these husbands the bulk of their salary became personal mad money. Some might give a standard amount, usually under the actual needs, but that was pretty much that.

Now we would assume that most working adults get raises and bonuses from time to time, but hardly ever, these wives claim is that raise ever passed along to the family.

This again, may not win me any popularity points, but so it is. The Bible indicates that by divine assignment it is the role of the male (*where possible*) to be responsible for the family provisions. I add, '*where possible*', because situations can arise that may change the basic operating principles. If a husband becomes incapacitated, or loses his job, or is laid-off, the wife may become the major breadwinner temporarily, or even permanently. Yet, if this couple works as a team, it does not have to cause conflicts. Team members that win, work together!

Whatever the financial income, whether both spouses work, one spouse works, or one can't work, there needs to be an overall plan. A plan designed to move you toward the goals that have jointly been established. If something happens in the course of life that was not on the radar you make the needed adjustments and move on. The adjustment should not be too over- whelming because you should have in place a master plan that is flexible.

The method I often use when doing pre-married counseling or for new Couples, is to get people to answer, *"What do you want to be doing, and where do you want to be in ten years"*? I like to urge them to set a reasonable goal, then make plans how they will reach that goal. Looking backwards, what should they be doing in the ninth year of their ten year plan?

And what should they be doing in the fifth year and so on as we continue to look backwards? Then I ask them, *"What should you be doing tomorrow to advance that ten-year plan?"*

Don't set a goal that is so farfetched that one week later, or several months later, you become so frustrated, or disenchanted, that you abandon all hope. Reasonable is the way to go. When you are planning together your march to victory or how you are going to get there, remember you must build in a good system of measurement. Don't forget our first farmer. He chose a rifle that fired one shot at a time. He could only hit from the front one can at a time. If he missed, you would know it, just as certainly, as you would know when he hit. Farmer two could not possibly hope to measure his skill as a marksman, unless his goal was to hit everything in sight.

Some couples start out like our second farmer. If you were to ask them where they expect to land in several years, they might sound like they were wrapped in dreams. But with no reasonable target, and no system of measurement, they are just as likely to end up in a nightmare.

Earl saw his family plunge deeper and deeper in debt. After he got his sports car he felt he had to buy other things to support his new image. He paid less and less attention to the regular ongoing bills. He figured that Tammy would pick up the slack. Tammy had no idea that he expected her to find the money for the utilities. When she approached him, because of the shut-off notices, he didn't want to talk about it. In fact, he grabbed his coat and headed for the door. Later, they had a big blowout when he blamed his wife for their loss of phone and electrical services.

Several factors are evident. There could not have been much of a plan in the beginning of their relationship. They apparently never talked and came to an understanding when they were dating. If Tammy had realized what Earl's mind set was about finance, perhaps she would not have fallen in love and married. If Earl knew that Tammy expected him to be the major breadwinner and that all of his money had to be put in common with hers, perhaps he would have had second thoughts. With his kind of selfishness, and secretiveness about his money, he might have even considered being a confirmed bachelor.

We see now that these two people are mismatched in their thinking and planning. However, it is too late to ponder about that now. They are married. The problem is now; so, what can be done to make this mismatch work? If I were their counselor, I think the first approach would be to sit them down and find some basic common handles. Tammy is not without any personal fault, but I think the main offender here is Earl. So. I would try to find a positive launching place first.

> *"Earl, you and Tammy have had some real problems in your marriage. We are not here to punish, or assign blame, but in order to be honest and get to the real problem, we must reach in deeply to find some answers." "If we could bury all the past failures and make a promise that life for the two of you would take a new, great turn for the better; would you be interested?"*
> How could he not answer *"yes"* to a promise like that?

The next step is the same one that a parent would use in showing a young child the dangers of playing near a hot stove. You use pain as a teacher. You hold a little hand near enough to the heat that they can understand what *"hot"* means without really letting them get burned.

Once you have established what hot means you verbally only have to call out, *"hot"* when you see that child playing near a danger zone. This same relationship method of pain to pleasure can work with adults in trouble.

Here are some sample methods that might lead an adult to a learning moment:

> *"Earl, remember how it felt when you came home and found that there was no electricity in the house?' Do you remember that you found all the food in the refrigerator had spoiled? Dinner was impossible because the stove could not work. You had to use your last fifteen dollars to take Tammy and your little girl out to get something to eat. When you returned there of course were no lights and it was cold because the heater could not work." Remember you had to stay in that condition for over a month?" Tell me Earl, what do you think happened here?"* Now Earl might start out blaming his wife for not paying the bills on time and ignoring shut-off notices. That's all right for him to start there. *"Earl"*, I would ask, *"how much money do you set aside each month for the utilities?" What is your method for seeing that these bills are paid?"* Can you see my method working? I first had to establish what *"that"* is! Then I let the spouse nearest the blame feel a little of the heat so that some pain comes through. Then we are better ready to talk about developing a plan for keeping us away from the fire. If I would begin assaulting Earl and telling him how it's all his fault for not seeing to it that the bills are paid, I would be just repeating what I'm sure his wife already told him. What I am trying to do is help him yell *"Hot"* to himself, and then develop a plan. He probably felt that giving Tammy some money every week was the right thing to do. He, on the other hand, probably never sat down with her to figure out what their bills were and

where the money was to come from. If he can feel the pain and discomfort of past experiences and know how to plan away from them then we have made some progress.

We not only use pain as a teacher in this method, but pleasure as well. To reinforce the plan, we point him to the pleasure of developing a good plan and experiencing the great feeling of satisfying his family. He has established and maintained a feeling of well-being in that home. Their little girl looks at him through admiring eyes knowing that her daddy is strong and protective. His wife feels protected and loved because his plan is working.

After that first honeymoon trip is over, it is then time to get down to serious business, the serious business of taking your family from the dream to the reality. The reality is that life is an ever-changing quilt. Each little patch separately related to the whole, but often different in color and texture. Yet in all of these patches there must be a constant system of planning and adjustment to that planning. The goal of the quilt-maker is to produce a quilt. Each little patch must be sewn into the whole. It may take a different set of stitches to attach swatches of silk than those of velvet, or linen. [*Not being a student of the craft, I'm not sure just how sound my illustration is at this point, but I feel I'm right.*] However, in life's tapestry, or quilt each segment might have a different composition. The planning you did five years ago, more than likely, will need ongoing adjustments. The patches may differ, the stitches that hold them may differ, but the goal is to create a worthy quilt.

Roger and Tanya had planned their family life around Tanya's home-town. Their four children were all born there. Like many couples, they had some ups and downs, but just when everything seemed to straighten out and begin running smoothly, Roger's company location changed. Because of his area of expertise, the demand took them to live in several major cities around the country. This of course caused them to plan and re-plan before and after each move. They never took their eyes off of their basic goal. This staying on course has resulted in a successful family relationship.

Perhaps back when our grandparents were starting out, life could be lived simply, almost day to day. We cannot afford to live like that now. Planning almost daily is crucial to our successful operation. Some planning advocates recommend planning diaries that have spaces and lines for every 15 or 30 minutes during the day. Personally, I'm afraid of committing my whole day to a half-hour, by half-hour running sheet. Frankly, I think that it would look so ridiculous on paper that I'd be shocked, and you would believe it to be untruthful. Here's an example of what I'm talking about. One Sunday morning, following the sermon, I looked at my watch. It was about 1:30 P.M. I had to take a trip that I had timed before that would take one hour. I was to arrive at a dinner honoring two retired Pastors. 5:00 PM was to be my arrival time. The plan was to gather at 3:45 with the others going. I felt if someone was a little late, we could still make it if we left as late as 4 P.M. There were a few other thoughts on my mind, like running home and resting for an hour or so, or grabbing a snack to hold me over until dinner. Well, that Sunday, the Lord and my parishioners had other plans. I participated in six conferences and counseling sessions, back to back. I conferenced and counseled up to 4:00. It certainly was a marathon day.

Was this all in my plan? Well yes, and no. No, I didn't sit on the bed early that morning and pencil in appointments. What I did do is say to the Lord, *"This day belongs to you. Use me in it like you want to."* Now I grant you if I had to live every day like that I'd be in a lot of trouble. I did have a general idea of what I would be doing but not with every time slot on a list filled. In fact, as a happy people-server, I hate to serve with one eye on the clock. I try not to ever let people see me checking my watch on them. Yet we all know that life demands some obedience to time.

We have talked about setting goals. This planning not only involves what we do on an annual basis, but almost daily as well. I want to be an excellent pastor. The performance scores that people would give me at the end of a decade are made up of how I go about doing my work with them in their daily lives.

Now to return to an old point. Since this book is about marriages running right, don't forget the communication factor. Husbands and wives must sit and plan the rest of their lives together. These plans need ongoing revisions. It is important to make these revisions and changes together. Updates in one's thinking that are going to initiate a policy shift, or procedural changes must be communicated to your spouse. It should be presented with an open mind, and received with an open mind. The new direction should really be a possible new direction, that I feel strongly about. Let the other person know that you feel strongly about your idea, but that it can only be moved on with the approval and cooperation of both partners.

Be reminded that sometimes men and women communicate differently. Men usually think to themselves and somehow feel that as they were developing that plan their wives were made privy to on-going information. When his wife accuses him of shutting her out of his world he will have absolutely no idea of what she is talking about. For many years I have used the illustration of how we played and what we played with as an indicator of our communication skills. Chances are if you are a woman, you grew up with dolls and maybe even stuffed animals. There were a lot of play times when you had tea parties, played house, Doctor/Nurse and other games that mostly involved your toys and you. Ladies, since most of your toys represented some kind of life, there was verbal transmission. You probably talked for yourself and then answered in another voice for the doll. Think about it. There was a lot of verbal communication going on then!

Now, if you are a man, you perhaps had a different kind of toy. Probably you played more with inanimate kinds of toys. Boats, guns, tanks, spaceships, and other lifeless playthings would have provided hours of fun.

While the girl is engaged in chatty little kinds of social situations, the boy next door is making all kinds of bang-bang, growl and crush, and swish noises, as he moves his toys about. Even when his G. I. Joe men are used, it's likely in a war setting where conversations are short and the groans of battle are long. It is expected that cars, trucks, and earth moving equipment that don't have their own motor sounds be supplied with such, by us. I remember that it was very easy for me to learn to drive a standard shift car because I had the motor sounds in my head. I knew when to shift from first to second, and then to third, (*then we called it high gear*) and back again, simply by playing the sounds back in my mind. I guess psychologists somewhere might give it a fancy sounding term like, *"Good hand to auditory co-ordination rhythm"*. It says something about making sounds, but a good marriage needs more than a few grunts and groans.

The more I thought about my long-time illustration about our different Backgrounds, it starts in the communication game, I felt that something was missing. The illustration is a good one, but needs a deeper enhancement. If we are not careful, the point seems to be that females are verbally able to communicate and men are not. That's not where I want to go. Working with a number of couples having communication problems, I've discovered that many husbands accused of not communicating verbally, deny this. They believe that they do communicate. They do indeed talk about what's going on. The eye opener that came through is that this talking goes on legitimately, but it is done by men internally. Many men have a personal system that operates inside their mind. They are perfectly comfortable with it because they talk things over, make adjustments, come to conclusions, formulate solutions, and are over and done with it. Along comes this woman who accuses him of not communicating where he is coming from, and on top of it all, claims that she is frustrated by him. *"What is your problem,"* he says? He knows that he has talked it out, wasn't she listening?

Going back to our childhood toys, I think I can almost grasp a handle here. Her toys, coupled with her role-playing, concentrate on a sharing system of communication (*you talk, I talk*). His system does not call for any sharing of information. Often his thoughts are wrapped up in the internal grunt and groans that he makes while thinking about a problem, or situation.

Now we need to make a point very clear, not all men are poor communicators, and not all women are good communicators. My thoughts and illustrations are generalized. I've met and counseled women who were the ones causing the difficulties in their marriages by not sharing, honestly what was going on inside. It's hard to second-guess what a person might be thinking.

Latonia told me on the phone several times that she loved her husband and wanted their marriage to work. She got her husband to agree to come to counseling, but once there she refused to share the vital information locked up in her mind. Their marriage was failing and she very privately held the key. Jesse, her husband, became willing after a time to set goals and to aim for improvement. Unfortunately, it won't work when there is little or no cooperation. Scripture uses the illustration of an Ox and a jackass as pulling partners: An ox is a strong, broad animal that plods along with deliberate sure steps. The jackass on the other hand is unpredictable and heady, likely to start and stop at will. The reason that an ox and a jackass can't make it as a pulling team is that they both have opposite ideas of how the load should be pulled. If either one would just stop doing his own thing long enough to try the others' approach, their joint effort would work.

I recall sitting across from Latonia and Jesse with amazement as she sat with stone like stubbornness refusing to give even a hint of the love she had confessed to have for her husband on the phone. During a recess, I asked her if she loved Jesse. *"Yes, I do,"* was her reply, but she, for whatever reasons, never confessed this love to her husband. In fact, she seemed to go out of her way to be hateful and uncooperative. One word of admission to loving him could have helped save their marriage. Whatever she felt inside, remained there. Jesse obviously had hurt her, but unless one is willing to open up and expose hurt, pain, disappointment, anger, and frustration, even counseling is a lost cause.

Marriage is, in one sense, a business. It, like any business, runs on good management principles and practices. It will not run perpetually on its own without constant planning, operation, management, and evaluation. The moment that you set a goal you have to establish a system of measuring whether you are on or off target. When something is happening that is causing a lop-sided relationship, it's time for a meeting of the board.

The husband as the head of the family, is comparable to the chairman of the board. He is held responsible by God, for whatever is going on in the home, but don't think for one moment that that wife is without equal responsibility. In the words of Dr. Clarence Walker, a popular Marriage and family counselor in Philadelphia, "The husband is indeed the head of the marriage, but the wife should equal him in influence." The way that I have addressed this same concept through our seminar series is in the session on *"Authority and the Appeal"*: A husband may make a decision that won't wash well. His wife has the right of appeal.

(The two following examples, Esther and Abigail, will be used again in the next chapter to help us focus on the importance of the Appeal Process.)

For me, the greatest example of a successful appeal is found in the Old Testament book of Esther. Queen Esther put her life on the line to appeal to her husband-King for the lives of her Jewish people. Queen Esther's method is worth studying by every wife who wants to develop an effective appeal to her husband's authority.

The first thing she did was to realize that; *"The way to a man's heart (heart/mind) is through his stomach"*. I'm not sure if anyone knows just where that quote we hear so often comes from? But the validity of it seems to be well established. She must have had some insight that truly, *"The way you get the appeal started is with the meal you put in his stomach,"*

Esther fixed the King and Haman, her [*unrevealed enemy*] the finest meal possible. King Ahasuerus was so overwhelmed with her banquet, that he was ready to give her up to half of his kingdom to show her favor. Notice that Esther did not accept this generous offer because it was not in her objectives, based on her goal to win release for her people. Esther seized the moment, not to reveal her petition, but to invite her two admiring guests to Banquet II. In so many words she was saying, *"If you think today's cuisine was something, you haven't seen anything yet!"* Continuing to be overwhelmed with her banquet spread, King Ahasuerus again makes his offer of giving Queen Esther up to half of his kingdom. She then puts the pieces in place by revealing her enemy. Haman was trapped, and judgment swift! She could not spring her trap too early. It was important to secure the steadfast favor of Ahasuerus because he was often cruel, and heartless. Haman being so close to the king might have had a chance to twist and maneuver the situation to his advantage if she exposed her hand too soon. She used patience, and cunning, along with her skill for entertaining, to set the stage. She understood her husband's heart. Her appeal was not hurried.

Another successful appeal is found in 1 Samuel chapter 25. A wicked, rich landowner had lived all winter under the protection of David's army, camped in the surrounding hills. Prior to the army, bands of marauders used to swoop in and rob farmers and sheep owners. During the time of year when the sheep were sheared for wool and some prepared for food, David sent some messengers to ask for food provisions for his men. The answer he got from Nabal, the rich landowner, was a nasty, insulting refusal. *"Who is this David anyway? Who are these renegades in the hills? Am I to give food to every rebel that comes by?"* When David received the message, he was furious to say the least. He not only gave the word to destroy everything walking on this ungrateful fool's property, but strapped on his own sword to personally oversee the slaughter. That's some real, *"You made me mad"!*

One of history's greatest appeals came when news of the refusal Reached the ears of Abigail, Nabal's wife. She immediately knew that trouble would follow. She hastily gave orders to load up the pack animals (*they didn't have 18 wheelers in those days*) with one hundred clusters of raisins, two hundred loaves of bread, two skin flagons of wine, five measures of corn, two hundred cakes of figs, and 5 already dressed sheep. She gave orders to ship them Express mail- with same day delivery. Not leaving anything to chance, she arrived right behind the goods.

Abigail's appeal showed that she knew something about a man's nature and perhaps even a little about David's character as well. She appealed to David not to do that thing that he had purposed in his heart to do. She let him know that he had the reputation of being a good man, a fair man, and a just man. She appealed to him not to tarnish his image with revenge to such as the likes of Nabal. She expressed that Nabal's name meant foolish, and that he was living up to every syllable of it. *"Why soil your hands with scum,"* would be her words set to our modern expression? She read David's heart and provided a viable alternative that did not compromise his manhood. She understood the ways of a man and skillfully worked with that understanding.

Abigail's appeal method first recognized David's basic need of food for himself, And his men. After taking care of the basic needs, she next developed her appeal platform. She began by affirming that he was in a position of power and authority over her. She acknowledges that her life was in his hands. She even acknowledges that her husband's life is in his hands, but challenges him that killing Nabal would be worthless because it would soil David's great reputation. In modern words it would sound like this. *"You have the power and might to kill him, but why would you even waste your time on a fool whose greatest goal in life is to measure up to his name, that already means foolish?" Smart gal to say the lease!*

This would certainly get my attention. She built David up, agreed to his power and might, and then opened up a desirable alternative. This is the way of a strong appeal.

The reason that many wives fail in getting their husbands to choose to do the best thing, is that they play the role of the spoiler, or the adversary. The spoiler is the one that says every idea is a bad one. *"That won't work!" "That's so stupid"! "You'll do it without me!"* The adversary type is the one who undermines everything that the husband says and does. She jumps ahead making decisions, and insulting him, until he no longer cares what she does. Once a husband reaches the, *"I don't care,"* stage, his sense of self-worth has already hit low voltage. Actually, the *"I don't care,"* is a kind of a defense mechanism at first. A device to let him keep face within. Remember, most men have strong egos on the outside, but are very much at risk on the inside. We will look more in depth at the male role related to authority in the next chapter.

Understanding the make-up of your spouse, and just how that make-up fits into the plan of God, is important. Many marriages today could be working on a much greater level if these couples would stop and regroup God wants marriages to work! He has already provided a plan for it to work. It is not a matter of seeking if it is His will for it to work. It actually delights Him to see it working well. It brings glory to Him!

CHAPTER 7

WHO'S IN CHARGE

It cost you eighty bucks a piece for tickets. The nationally acclaimed philharmonic orchestra is on stage but this is certainly not what you paid for. This was to be your wedding anniversary treat. Treat indeed! For at least fifteen minutes you've been sitting and listening to a bunch of musicians play up and down the scale! It almost sounds like they are in some kind of musical war. Just as you begin to convince yourself to develop a plan to ask for your money back, out steps a gentleman in tails who strides to a little raised platform. He steps up and raises his hands, one holding a baton. He signals silence by tapping on a stand, pauses, then swings into motion. The orchestra follows and responds to his every move. Out from these once scattered musicians, bent on fighting each other with their instruments fifteen minutes ago, now flow sounds of harmonic beauty; a beauty that seems to reach down into ones very soul. Wow! What has happened here? What Changed?

In actuality, the orchestra was just loosening up until the one in charge took over. When direction was furnished, harmony with precision flowed. If there was no appointed leader and the musicians tried to follow themselves, chaos would follow. The leader needed to be present, and visible for it to work.

One of the questions on the pre-marriage form I use for eager couples asks, *"in marriage, who should be the boss"?* It is interesting to me that almost never does a member of our congregation get it wrong. The percentage of outside persons is not quite as high. If you answered that there are no bosses in the marriage relationship you are right! If you answered as some have, that it is the husband, you've got some home-work. I must admit although we have had some answer incorrectly that the man was the boss, I don't recall anyone ever answering that it was the woman.

In the labor force a boss can hire and fire. In the marriage relation-ship no one hires or fires! Try it and you will lose! A boss can give orders in the market place, but this will not work in a marriage relationship. However, the husband's biblical job description does put him in a leadership role. That role makes him answerable to God for what goes on in the family. We could never see him as a boss with that description but rather as a facilitator directly answerable to God. In Genesis 3 when the first family messed up, God made a house call. The first and only name He called was "Adam"! The Bible's assignment of being the family head is not easy. It carries with it the weight of the decisions made. Being family head does not mean that the man is the smartest, or the most gifted one. More often, the woman thinks and acts more quickly. she can often size up the problem, call in the workmen and get the job finished while her husband may still be thinking about it. What could work best is if the teammates could get together and use the best of both approaches. Men tend to be a little more thorough in their planning, if they would plan! What frustrates most wives is that they are not convinced that we are actually doing any planning. A typical example might be that Mary sees a crack in the wall beginning at the ceiling working its way down halfway to the floor. After months of asking John to deal with it, she calls in "MR. JOBBER" the local contractor to give her an estimate on patching and painting. Because she called his estimate might be a little higher to begin with. Mr. Jobber is interested in satisfying his lady customer who asked for, "patch and paint". So, patch and paint is what he will deliver. John, on the other hand, is not as likely to be as excited about the prospects of a paint job. Because of how he is wired, he's most likely trying to figure out what caused the crack. Is something wrong with the chemical composition of the old plaster, or is the house settling in that area? Is there structural damage? John knows that if there is a basic problem source, no amount of paint will solve it. It will reoccur in a few years. To paint and patch ignoring the source of the problem, to John is a waste of time and money. Mary hardly cares about problem source. She is tired of the eyesore. It is certainly worth it to her to spend the money to get rid of the aggravation. *"If it reoccurs, we'll just have to deal with it then."* Whether Mary's approach is right or wrong, John is responsible for seeing that some appropriate solution is worked out in a timely way. Wow men, that stings!

A man that goes around just making decisions and not following up on the consequences that come with those decisions isn't doing it right yet. It is easy to make a statement, introduce a policy, or initiate an action, but has that decision been thought out? What happens all along the line with the action? Is there a plan *"B"* if things don't work out? There may need to even be a plan *"C"* too.

Another thing about decisions in the family is that they should be fair. They should be designed to benefit everyone in the family, not just the head. I heard about a pastor one time that said that his family was going to have to live without spending a lot of money. He was not broke, but he just felt that was how they should live. And I think it was more "they"—the other members of the family. He liked to look nice, but when it came to the wife and kids, *"they"* had to *"Economize"!* His wife's shoes were often run-over, and her dresses never new. The children had to sort of share clothing. Shoes just got handed down the line. I don't think any of this was because the church was not paying him. This man was just plain stingy and selfish, and what made it worst, he didn't even feel that he had to live by the policy he set. He certainly, in violation of scripture, caused his children to exhibit wrath. His wife of all those years walked out on him when he needed her the most. He was actually left with the one he—had valued the most—himself!

When decisions are made for the benefit of one individual, it is usually the one most influential in the decision-making process. Those one sided decisions cause others discomfort. The *'Head of the family,'* is the leader whose job it is to look to the needs of the entire family. Headship connotes responsibility, not ownership. If we break it down further, we see that a worthy husband is a protector, defender, provider, initiator, and an encourager. When problems occur, it is the job of the head to try to bring things to a solution.

In our family, Mom is the major cook. Now, I can cook, (*at least back in the day*) but the family does not recognize me as the one responsible for the day-to-day food decisions in our kitchen. Yet, if the food budget is falling seriously short in contrast to the time left in the week, I have to get involved. If our food runs out on Wednesday and we've got several days left, they will stand outside of my door with strike signs. Everyone recognizes that we have a problem and they all know who has the responsibility to see that things get right. Perhaps enough money was not allocated from the beginning, or money was spent more on needed cleaning items and supplies than on actual food or maybe the wrong store was chosen, or food prices have sharply increased, etc. Whatever the reason, the head must become the investigator, not to blame, but to try to find a way.

From the very beginning of the marriage, the husband must erect a strong protective force around the family unit. This force is not just concerned with the physical alone, but gives equal weight to the spiritual and mental as well. This force might further be described as a protective climate. It sets perimeters, or borders around the family unit that work to guard against negative forces coming from two directions, forces breaking in, and forces breaking out. To go outside of those protective borders is to court real danger to the product. Just as dangerous is to allow those borders to be penetrated from without. In either case, there is danger to the fabric either by weakening or by risking contamination.

When we got married, one protective system decision we made was that we would not allow any outside force, source, or institution, with the exception of God, to invade our joint desire to set, abide by, or be directed by our own will. We felt we needed to know God's will first, and foremost. Then we could develop and set our will accordingly.

When Dennis and Alba got married, the borders around their marriage were never carved in stone. Perhaps Alba had some ideas of what should and should not be influencing their family, but not Dennis. He wandered in and out, trying this and that with very little idea of what boundaries should exist. He felt that it was fine for them to develop separate friends. He encouraged Alba to be friendly with some people who were quite different from her background training. She was very uncomfortable with these people. Soon, the walls of their marriage began to crumble. Nothing was stable or concrete anymore. Dennis wanted them to be flexible with no absolutes. He, as the head of the family failed to discipline his interests and some of his behavior. One summer night he couldn't sleep, he said, so he got dressed and said he was going out for a walk to cool off. Three hours later he came in the house as if nothing happened. When Alba challenged him about his whereabouts, he confessed that he went into a local bar to watch television. *"Bar—Television!"* she screamed, *"Are you nuts? You get out of bed at 1 AM to go for a walk and end up spending three hours watching television in a bar? Dennis, what is wrong with you?"* Little by little, Alba felt that she could not trust him to protect her, and to protect their initial dream. He did not allow what should have been a protective climate to hold him securely inside. Their marital walls were weakened by the behavior patterns from within.

The Browns on the other hand allowed their walls to be invaded from sources and forces outside. Cheryl got involved with a steady diet of daytime soaps. She began to allow certain ideas and practices to creep into her mind. Once, she trusted her husband without any doubts. Later, after getting hooked on the soaps, little by little she began to entertain suspicions about his faithfulness. These suspicions did not come because he had actually given any cause. Cheryl was just into the television world too much.

Patrick was so impressed with a couple of the guys on his job. They were into a social-cultural action club that was always doing something. Patrick wanted to adopt the life style of these people. In order to fit into this New World, he and Cheryl would have to change a few of the values that they held. *"Nothing major"*, Patrick said. One of these not so major things was alcohol. Drinking began to creep into his life-style. Maybe a beer after work, or a cocktail at the frequent office luncheons. Next, Patrick wanted Cheryl to begin having dinner parties for these new friends. Because of her unhealthy diet of soap operas, she did, at first, fantasize a bit about decorating, and entertaining in a high style. After a while, her church background began to make her feel uncomfortable about these parties, and what went on there. First, Patrick engaged in social-type drinking, but more and more it began to escalate. Soon, Patrick couldn't come home until he stopped by *"The Gents Club"*, a local tavern where professional types hung out. The toll began to weigh heavily on their marriage. Both had allowed their walls to be penetrated.

In both situations, with the Browns and the Turners, the walls of protection became seriously cracked and damaged. Dennis went out on his own seeking pleasures and new experiences. The Browns fell into a worldly trap and became infected. The results are the same. The Bible warns that we are to avoid worldly lust, shun the appearance of evil, and not to imagine a vain thing.

When outside things are brought into the marriage relationship, they will more than likely cause changes. This is true not only about negative influences but positive ones as well.

When a couple begins to be influenced by biblical principles, a positive, healthy difference can be experienced. The problem is often that so few people are exposed to those biblical principles that affect marriage.

Let's spend some time examining, understanding, and learning to work with a few of these principles related to who's in charge of what.

We find that in the Bible the husband has been appointed as the family head. Unfortunately, many have misunderstood, and misapplied that appointment.

Headship does not mean *"Boss"*, or ownership. A boss can hire, and fire, and direct all of the profits to himself if he wants to and more. Headship in the marriage is much like the pastor of a church. The Church belongs to God, not the pastor or the people! God has given it to them as a family like system, and structure. The pastor is a facilitator aiming to affect and carry out policy to enhance, encourage, maintain and advance the positive causes of the congregation. They should seek his agreement, direction, cooperation, and leadership as a representative of God. That pastor with all of that awesome responsibility still stands answerable to God.

The only one who could be *"Boss"* in the marriage is God! He can hire, and fire, and direct all of the glory to Himself, if He wants too. If we check out Adam in the garden, we can get some indications about the role of Headship. His assignment was to name the animals, tend to their well-being, dress the garden, etc. We see him as administrator, tender and vinedresser. After the fall, another part of the assignment is seen. He is the one directly answerable to God for the behavior and actions of the family.

We see God holding Adam responsible for all the actions going on in the garden. *"Adam, where are you?"* In modern terms, *"Adam, what's going on, and why do you feel you have to hide? What is going on?"* If we add up all of the goings on in the first three chapters of Genesis we see the husband as head in at least five overlapping areas:

1. *He is the administrative assistant to God. (God creates life; we can only give assistance in managing it.)*
2. *He is the local policy setter (based on the master policy authored by God).*
3. *He is the spokesperson answerable to God for the welfare and well-being of the family.*
4. *He is the responsible provider.*
5. *He is the local family protector.*

The husband as major policy setter also comes with responsibilities for the results of these policies. Some men set policy, but fail to take on the burden of following it up. Some policy decisions need to be amended, or even dropped. A man that cannot admit when he is wrong, and make appropriate changes, does not have it all together yet.

Terrence often made decisions that plunged his family deeper and deeper into debt. He wanted extra, but failed to provide extra. When the bill collectors called, he was not at home, so his wife took the heat. Their living room set was actually repossessed by a furniture company that was tired of getting the run-around. There were, sofa, two easy chairs, and an end table, all lined up on the side walk, neighbors gawking . . . Terrence was not home from the second shift so he missed the embarrassment that his wife and child felt. When he got home, he blamed his wife for not making the payments. *"I work hard all week and give you money to run this house. Can't you just pay these bills? What do you do with all the money anyway?"* No mention that the money given was far short of the need!

When the family head likes to set policy, but fails to follow it up, or take responsibility, it places an unfair burden on the wife. Giving the *"little woman"* the assignment and the authority to write checks might sound like the best management system, especially if she's better at it. However, not jointly shared, it could be the coffin nail to the marriage. The husband may indeed delegate the job of keeping the books to his wife, who he feels does it better. However, wisdom and experience teaches us that if he drops it on her and takes off for high ground she eventually will feel violated and unprotected. She needs to feel that even if she is the check writer, her husband cares what is happening. Most men are built to take the burden of administration. Notice I used the term, *"Built to take"*. I did not say that women couldn't be good administrators; that would be a dumb statement. What I am suggesting is that the make-up of most men is such that they can shoulder the administrative loads better.

The husband is just like the President of the U.S.A. who may give congress or some agency the power to sign a check, but he must shoulder the responsibility if that effort goes crazy. Some will remember the Watergate conspiracy. President Nixon resigned in embarrassment, not because he actually, sat down and planned the break-in, or even knew about it. His guilt came in two ways. Everyone remembers that he tried to cover up the wrongdoing, but few remember that the greater evil was that he allowed and encouraged the kind of climate that developed a plan that overzealous followers felt would be approved of. For whatever reasons, coverage, guilt, embarrassment, etc. he took the responsibility and resigned.

If the wife handles the money in the family because she is the best at it, please husband don't abandon her in the job. You need to be just as aware of what is going on financially as she. I recommend regular sessions where current, past and future finances are shared, especially when she writes the checks. This helps to reassure her that she is not out there alone to sink, or swim on her own. This advice should also prove helpful if the man writes the checks. Should something happen that causes the wife to step in to take over the financial reins, she should have some idea of where to begin.

Recently, I heard a famous husband/wife track team interviewed. The husband was the coach and the wife the track star. The interviewer wanted to know how disputes over a particular technique or approach would be handled. The husband said that each of them had a 49% vote that would be brought to the table for discussion. Two percent, he said, *"was left on the shelf. In the event that we don't agree I reach back and get that 2 % that is reserved for me and make the final decision."* He was not trying to be heady, or arrogant, as he simply explained that his job was to coach at that point. He not only had to see her point, and be fair to her, but also see the over-all condition and position relating to the situation, hopefully to make the wisest choice. This is probably a good place to plug in the reminder again of the appeal process factor.

A lot of men feel that once they've made up their mind on a matter that is it! They have chosen the way to go. May I remind husbands that that is not always the end of the matter. There is another step left in the decision making process called, *"The Appeal"*. The appeal is the wife's right to submit, or resubmit evidence that when examined, may lead to altering the decision. If you husbands have trouble accepting this step, or taking it seriously, I might remind you that you married your wife because you felt incomplete without her! Your life was just that, and you knew it! Now that you have her to complete your life don't close down your blessing pretending to yourself that all decisions are masterfully manufactured in your limited headspace, never to be questioned. You, like me, are not that good! Often through the appeal process a potentially bad situation is saved.

We visited Queen Esther in the previous chapter but there is so much to be learned, please allow me to return there to make some additional points. The Queen was faced with a life-threatening problem. Some enemies of her people (the Jews) had convinced the King to decree a bad law. On a certain date all of the Jews could be set upon and killed without penalty to the killer. In fact, the killer was permitted to claim the victim's property. The author of this plan was a man named Haman, an advisor to the King. Esther had to devise a plan to get the King to change this wicked law. The King no doubt trusting Haman did not really think it through. Once he had signed it into law it could not be reversed, according to laws of the Medes and Persians, but something had to be done to save her people.

According to the Royal system, no one without expressed invitation could gain entrance to see the King, including the queen unless the King held out his golden scepter, signifying acceptance. Should he refuse, the uninvited visitor could be executed on the spot. Taking a chance on his mood swings Esther made it by the first hurdle, for the scepter was gladly extended to her. Her appeal was not revealed at that time, but rather a dinner invitation was extended to King Ahasuerus and his head prince, Haman. So gracious and charming was this invitation that it was accepted without a pause. Haman was beside himself with joy that he should be so honored to be included in a special dinner invitation with the King, prepared by the Queen.

Queen Esther put on one fine banquet. Perhaps this is where we get the expression, *"A banquet fit for a King"*. I'm not sure how she fixed his grits and greens but they must have been something else! Wives take notice that at this point the King was ready to give her whatever she wanted, but she did not rush into it. She was so smooth! She had a plan, and she was working her plan. The Queen asked the King to come to another dinner, and to bring Haman back. Once again Haman was overjoyed that the queen should so honor him to eat with the King at her house. He couldn't see that set up was in the works.

The second banquet was even better, if that was possible. The King had been well pleased by the great meal and again promised to grant her request. It was then that she lowered the boom on Haman, telling of his devilish plan. King Ahasuerus was so angry about this latest news that he had to take a walk outside to think. In the meantime, Haman sprang up to appeal to the queen for mercy. He must have lost his balance and fell on the bed where Esther was reclining. It was at this point that the King returned finding Haman fallen upon the queen's bed. It must have looked like a rape attempt. Haman and his family were about to become execution history for sure!

We can learn several things from Esther's appeal. First, notice that she took her time making her appeal. Her plan seemed to be well thought out. Notice even before that she did not go out of the process. She cooperated with the established procedure. She honored her husband never trying to rush him into favoring her. Next, she was ready to present an alternative plan that would not compromise his best interests. She did not complain and nag him to do something-she offered a viable option. Some women might have used the opportunity to criticize their husbands for being tricked into signing such a silly law in the first place. Since no one would criticize the King, in this case it's a moot point, but I get the idea that Esther would have presented it in much the same fashion. It was also evident that her attitude said, *"I will abide by whatever decision you make"*. Finally notice that she treated her husband with fancy favor. She really put on a fancy spread. This action said to Ahasuerus, *"You are very special to me. Your decision is worth courting"*.

The appeal process is valid. It should be used with a spirit of cooperation and sensitivity. It is an attempt to look at a situation from a different perspective, or through a new pair of eyes. We might look at Daniel and the Hebrew boys' appeal to their Supervisor, The Prince of the King's Eunuchs. They felt that eating the foods of the new land, (actually meat and wine from the King's table) where they were being held in captivity would ultimately prove harmful to their strong bodies. Instead of telling the prince that the special food they served was junk, they suggested to him an experiment. See for 10 days if pulse, a simple vegetable diet they were accustomed to eating would make them stronger, with better complexions. Melzar's neck was on the line because he was responsible for their well-being. If they were to look like their health was failing, his head would roll. But because their appeal was based on a reasonable trial period that he could evaluate, it became attractive. Ten days certainly could not hurt them drastically. If it worked and they looked better than the other youths, his stock would go up. The appeal worked—the experiment worked! If we review these two illustrations, several strong suggestions for making an appeal are seen:

1. *Try not to hurry an appeal, take your time, and let him know he is very special and that his decision is worth you courting, and that it deserves your best thought.*
2. *Let your husband know that you honor and respect his responsibility.*
3. *When presenting an alternative plan, do not compromise his best interest, or belittle the former plan.*
4. *Offer a viable option; sometimes some of the previous operating options can be included in the new plan to be considered.*
5. *Assure your husband that no matter the final decision, you plan to abide by his best judgment.*
6. *Out of the experience of Daniel, we see another strong suggestion. An agreement to review and evaluate the new plan shortly after it has begun.*

During a recent marriage seminar, the question came up about the possible disqualification of a husband to be respected as the head. Does God expect the wife to follow her husband's lead even to their destruction? This is an excellent question but the answer is not as clear-cut. The first scriptural example that comes to mind is that of Abraham and Sarah. Abraham told his wife Sarah to shade the truth in order to save their lives as they journeyed into a strange land. He told her to tell these new people that she was his sister. She was very beautiful and Abraham was afraid that they would kill him if they knew he was her husband. She did as he instructed and still Peter says she called him lord! That is some real faith. Most women would not follow their man that far. Yet still she was blessed even though she lied. So, it would seem that even if the husband were wrong, the wife is covered.

I'm not sure however, that the story ends with that illustration. In another passage of scripture, we see Abigail ignoring her wicked husband and actually, saving their lives and the lives of their servants, plus the reputation of Captain David, who was about to destroy all. It would seem that each situation stands on multiple factors. Abraham's venture was probably not life threatening. He made a bad decision, because he was fearful and did not know what else to do. He felt that he was trying to save their lives. His intent was not to do harm. There was no hatred or malice in his actions.

Nabal, on the other hand, was a mean, arrogant, selfish man. He didn't care about anyone else apart from his own good. For months David and his army had camped up in the hills above Nabal's shepherds. Because of the strong army presence, the bands of marauders were discouraged from attacking the flocks. It was like having his own private army without cost! David, in all that time neither took, or asked anything from Nabal. When sheep shearing time came around, the provisions for the men had run very low. So, David sent some of his young men to ask for some provisions. Nabal's reply was like telling David to get lost! *"Who is this David?" "Am I to give out of my wealth to every vagabond or panhandler who comes to my door begging?"* So, he turned the men away abruptly. When Abigail, who was not home, found out, she immediately went to the pantry and loaded up every pack animal she could put her hands on. Loaves of bread, skins of wine, clusters of grapes, cakes of figs, parched grain, and five sheep already dressed to eat were loaded on and sent to David. Next, she mounted her beast and made haste to make an apology in person. She actually made a brilliant appeal to a man other than her husband. The appeal was effective. Please read the complete story account in I Samuel 25:1-42.

Why was it all right for Abigail to go against her husband's decision? Does not the Bible teach that the wife is covered by her husband, thus implying danger to her if she moves from his protective force? This is true to a point. The Lord never said that women have to shut down their brains and become robots in order to follow their husbands.

If a man begins to make decisions and demands that are purely selfish, and without regard to the welfare and safety of the wife (and/or children) I feel that we are looking at a possible exception. Especially when this type of behavior becomes a harmful pattern.

One dear lady became very angry with me when in a marriage seminar; the subject of authority and appeal came up. I think that she felt that I was saying that a wife had to follow her husband's lead no matter what. *I don't believe that!* She was particularly disturbed because I pointed out that the Bible says to women to be subject to their own husband. It does not say, *"Christian husband".* Many churches teach incorrectly that if the husband is unsaved, the saved wife does not have to listen to him. That is utter foolishness. The principle operates the same, saved, unsaved, knowledgeable, or ignorant! This is why we strive so hard to tell women to marry a man who is already under the Lord's authority. Otherwise, he is given by God authority to be her head, but he himself is outside of God's will for his own personal life. That unsaved husband does have the God-given authority to say to that wife, *"I don't want you to go to that church anymore."* It is crazy, but while God would not agree with his foolish decision, He, at the same time, endorses his right to make it. Now I did not say that God didn't have His way of getting back at that foolish husband. He pays back to be sure!

Laban Deid, Sr. was a decorated Vietnam Veteran. When he came home from war, his family began to notice changes in him. He started withdrawing himself from people. Next, he started insisting that Ediba, his wife also withdraw herself from people. He did not want her to have anything to do with her neighbors, her family, and finally her church. Ediba, wanting to please her husband and be submissive to him, after a while, agreed to break off outside contact with the people she cared about. Pastor Goodfellow counseled her, for a time, to follow her husband's lead. *"God knows your heart. He knows that you have a mind to worship Him. Laban preventing you from coming is not going to un-save you.*

See what God wants to do through here. Time will reveal what is the proper course to follow. Pray much, and the congregation will pray. Remember that God will in time reveal what is right"!

When after a reasonable period of time and Laban's behavior had not improved, Ediba felt that she could no longer abide under the present circumstances. He wanted her to remain in the house with almost no contact with the outside world. His job had to lay him off because he was causing problems with the other workers. They began getting notices for delinquent bills. Things rolled steadily downhill quickly. *"Let me go back to the people of God"*, she pleaded one night. *"They love me, I need them. I miss them so very badly."* *"No"! he screamed; "I hate them. Hypocrites, busybodies, meddlers, No!"* *"Laban, I've been faithful to your wishes, often against my better judgment, but this is ridiculous! It is taking us nowhere. We have no one! No family contact, no church family, I can't take this any longer".*

It was clear after a time that Laban Deid was out of control! It was clear that his wife could not follow his leadership any longer. His behavior was unreliable, irresponsible, and erratic. To trust his judgment further was to bring total destruction to the entire family. She then took matters into her hands. If recovery were to occur, it would have to be on new terms. He had disqualified himself as the family head. Was this position lost forever? Not necessarily, but he would certainly have to earn the right to assume leadership again.

Gail faced a similar situation in her home. Not being cut off or isolated from friends, loved ones, or church members, but Larry had messed up big time! He had invested large amounts of their savings in several shaky business deals. His job relocated to Mexico, and he was unemployed. Out of frustration, he gambled away the remaining funds causing Gail to go back to work, while still raising their children. She tried to go along with him as best she could, even when he started drinking. The drinking then got heavier. Finally, she had to take over because Larry had disqualified himself as their leader. Gail tried hard to keep the image of her husband as family head intact, especially in front of their three children. Things, however, just kept spiraling downhill.

So then when, scripturally, does the wife have the right to take over the leadership? I believe there is no controversy when a husband is stricken down physically by sickness, and certainly by death, that the wife is certified by God to lead that family. The widow of one of the sons of the prophets, Elimelech, whose wife *Naomi*, Mother-in-law of *Ruth*, both supply *examples of wives taking over for their deceased husbands*. I don't think that we have to stretch greatly in our thinking to understand that if these husbands were unable to take care of business because of a grave illness, i.e. coma, paralysis, etc. that this would press the wife into duty. If we can understand and accept the former position, isn't it also reasonable that if a husband becomes mentally unable, emotionally unable, and perhaps socially/politically imbalanced to make proper decisions for the family that he disqualifies himself?

When Abigail took matters into her own hands, it was because she realized that Laban's decision had jeopardized the lives of all who were associated with him. Striking words had come to her through the lips of one of her young servant men. (I Samuel 25:17) *"Now therefore know this and consider what you should do; for evil is determined against our master and against all his house. And he is so ill-natured that one cannot speak to him."* Here is the formula:

1. *Know the history, and condition of the situation, or problem.*
2. *Consider what must be done to keep evil from devastating, or destroying, or hampering the progress of the family.*
3. *Seek God's leading and take the necessary action.*

Even the young servant pointed out that Laban was out of control. *"He is so ill-natured that no one can speak to him".*

Please don't get me wrong. I am not trying to encourage wives to slide out from under their husband's protective covering. What I am saying is that there are those, I hope, rare situations that become so crucial because of *a husband who is out of control that I believe* **there is a point at which he disqualifies himself as a family leader!**

Sometimes very unwise church groups will tell a woman who is being physically abused by her husband that she has to remain in that abusive situation in order to be blessed by God. My dear fellow pastors, counselors, and other spiritual leaders, there is no blessing there! Her life may be hanging in the balance. That husband needs help! That wife needs help! At that point, they cannot help each other.

Headship over the wife never carries with it the ability to punish physically, or otherwise. The husband if he is a father is never the father of his wife, even if she calls him *"Daddy"*. I once heard of a pastor who believed in whipping his wife. **That's sick!** I feel that he not only disqualified himself as her husband, but the pulpit as well. What could he preach about, and to whom? In that case, some of the brethren needed to step to him. I wonder how manly he would be at that point. Rest assure, there is no scripture or combination of scriptures that would support that kind of behavior. Please, any woman caught up in an abusive situation, ***get away first, and then and get help!***

Sometimes there are indicators during courtship. I recall watching on television the story of a former Miss America who later revealed that she had an abusive boyfriend. He was jealous and hot-tempered.

The first time he went into a rage and hit her, he apologized profusely. He assured her that it would never happen again. She should have made that statement true, as she took off for safety and total, permanent separation. Unfortunately, she did not make the break and it just got worse. If during the courting period, you see shades of abuse coming, break and run! Telltale signs of uncontrolled anger accompanied by throwing things, punching or kicking things, cursing, screaming, etc., should not be taken lightly. If a man does that and he's just dating you, what will he do when he thinks he owns you? Also, these same telltale signs when they appear in a young woman you are dating, men, end it!

There are some females out there who have decided that they have the right to throw punches and other things because they can get away with it. They have reminded their men, *"You can't hit a woman in this town"*. Well, all of the hitting should have been left on the playground, and school yards, etc. when you were growing up. We were not designed by God to be physical, mental, or verbal punching bags. When God has truly joined us together as man and wife, love gently guards and guides our roles. I close this chapter with these beautiful words from I Corinthians 13, translated from several sources:

> *Verse 1: Though I speak with the tongues of men and angels but have not love (KJV) [that reasoning, intentional, spiritual devotion . . . inspired by God for and in us] I am only a noisy gong or a clanging symbol (amplified).*

> *Verse.2: Even if I speak God's word and know every kind of hidden truth and have every kind of knowledge (Beck), and though I have all faith, so that I could remove mountains (KJV), but have not love, I am nothing (RSV)*

> *Verse.3: Even if I give away all that I have to feed the hungry (Beck), If I were burned alive for preaching the Gospel (Taylor) but have not love, I gain nothing (RSV).*

> *Verse.4: This love of which I speak is slow to lose patience—it looks for a way of being constructive (Phillips). Love never boils with "jealousy. It never boasts, is never puffed with pride;*

> *Verse 5: Does not act with rudeness, or insist upon its rights; (Williams) not quick to take offense, love keeps no score of wrongs,*

> *Verse 6: Does not gloat over other men's sins. (NEB) but always glad when truth prevails*

> *Verse 7: Always slow to expose, always eager to believe the best, always hopeful.*

> *(Moffatt Trans.) It gives us power to endure everything (Williams Trans.)*

Verse 8: Love will never come to an end (NEB) the time will come when we outgrow prophecy (Knox Trans.) As for tongues, they will cease; as for knowledge, it will pass away. (RSV)

Verse 9: For we know in part, and we prophesy in part. (KJV)

Verse 10: When wholeness comes (NEB) then that which is in part shall be done away.

Verse 11: When I was a child, I spoke as a child, I understood as a child, but when I became a man, I put away childish things.

Verse 13: And now these three faith, hope, and love, go on, but the most important of these is love. (Beck Translation)

CHAPTER 8

ESSENTIAL PARTNERING

Ecclesiastes 4:9-12 says:

9 Two are better than one, because they have a good reward for their labor.

10 For if they fall, one will lift up his companion. But woe to him who is alone when he falls, For he has no one to help him up.

11 Again, if two lie down together, they will keep warm; But how can one be warm alone?

12 Though one may be overpowered by another, two can withstand him. And a threefold cord is not quickly broken.

NKJV

OUR FRIENDS TOM and Ella were jewelers on Philadelphia's exclusive *'Jeweler's Row'*. You've got to understand that to have a business on 'Jeweler's Row' one must conduct *real business!* We're not talking about the kind of operation where one goes into business, but rather where one decides to build a business. People go into business and sometimes right out of business overnight. They fail for lack of planning, lack of commitment, or a lack of understanding the principles of business management. Anyone of which will sink a business venture but often it is a combination of things missing.

People who build a business take a lifetime. Dr. C. Milton Grannum explains it this way. *"People who go into business plan to spend the first dollars they make right away. Those who build a business plan for their offspring to eventually prosper and spend from that business."* He illustrates that those just going into business often justify their need for a brand-new car almost right after they've hung out their sign. *"The look is good for business,"* they say. Some people even feel compelled to move to a better neighborhood, again, almost right away to help the *'look of business'*.

The interesting thing about Tom and Ella is that they were partners in everything. They worked life together! Tom, who has since gone on to be with the Lord, worked his way up from an apprenticeship to a proud Jeweler. He studied his craft well learning everything that he could from his employers who became his mentors. When these mentors saw his brilliance and tenacity they began entrusting more and more responsibility to him. From apprentice to sales manager to owner, he climbed. Now his rise might seem remarkable to some, and it certainly was, but to Tom he was only working on his expectations. In other words, he planned to be successful. It was not a surprise to him! It came from hard work and a solid business background. He came from a business family where he learned the principles of business from his father, whose business continued to run successfully led by his mother after her husband passed away. A stable well-run business based on partnership should be able to withstand the absence of a partner because it should be based on business principles rather than personality alone.

What Tom learned about the jewelry business he taught to his wife. His wife's skills were in organization and management. Together they forged a tightly run family business. Their business eventually included their adult children who were brought up on the same principles of business. The jewelry business has continued to do well even after the parents retired. **Success comes in building layer upon layer and step by step, with patience and discipline** as very important factors.

For the last several years in our marriage workshops we have been circulating and collecting a survey to determine the needs of our attendees so that we could better prepare materials to answer their questions and needs. It began at a seminar we were doing for pastors and wives and continued for a while in our regular seminars. To my surprise the overwhelming request was for information on partnering. *"Just how do you become partners"*, was their question? I have a feeling even though it was decades ago, this question is still a current concern. So, let me begin here developing an answer to this question about partnering.

I believe that most of the positive principles and practices experienced among business partners are pretty much the same with marriage partners. In business, partners must have a common goal and common objectives. The same is true in successful marriage partnerships. Business partners must recognize that each partner has a unique strength to bring to the relationship. This is just as true in marriage relationships as well. In one of our 6 pre-marriage counseling sessions I now ask for each person to identify both their strengths and weaknesses. I want them to identify the strengths and weaknesses that will ultimately affect their new marriage.

Then the next question I ask them is to identify traits of weakness and traits of strength that they see in their potential partner. Marriage is no joke. You've got to be as aware as you can be of the good and the bad and sometimes the ugly. If they cannot identify any of the strengths or weakness in either or both categories, I quickly send up a red caution flag. There is either an honesty problem or a lack of marriage readiness. Either way caution is definitely needed.

In the Ecclesiastes passage, the advantage of two at labor is applauded for its good reward. If one falls down the other will lift up his fellow. Partnership is based on both having strengths and the partners being willing to share their strength. Strong marriages are based on the mutual needs of each partner. If I am strong in every area, which is unlikely, and my wife is just as weak as I am strong, the reliance element is missing. Good partnership has some trade-offs. An often-heard statement prior to divorce is, *"I don't need you anymore."* There seems to be a principle of reliance at work in strong vibrant marriages. This trait is seen in strong marriage *partners*. We must learn to rely on the strength of our partner, especially in the areas of our own lack of strength.

In our personal marriage I am a doer. Once I have prayed and feel the definite leading of God I am so on it! Bring out the horns, roll the drums and let's get it started in here. I am so often enmeshed in the doing of the vision that I'm not always thinking about on-going prayer for the project. I'm certainly not trying to be independent from God. On the contrary I am very reliant on Him. Understanding my spiritual make up, I just assume because of my faith that the blessing is already in place. I just expect to walk through walls.

My wife on the other hand begins to pray throughout the journey. She leaves nothing to human achievement. Her faith is in God working through her constant prayer. My faith is in God giving me the go-ahead sign. My weakness is definitely bolstered by her strength. It wasn't until recently when we were studying the prayer of Jabez that I discovered that seldom do I actually pray pointedly for my own personal success. Unless there is a specific need or something urgent I tend to pray generally for myself. I am much more pointed however when it comes to my family, congregation, ministry and the needs of others. Yet seldom am

I praying for personal achievement. I just kind of expect God to bless. And He certainly has done that. But remember, there is Dot covering every detail of my life with her prayer. **We are partners!**

Prayer for marriage partners is a must! We begin each day with prayer. I Depend on my wife's supportive prayer. I cannot imagine where I would be without them. In fact, I don't even want to imagine that thought. We know that I tend to be a dreamer. Dot's partnership in my dreams helps to give me the confidence I need to launch forward. Not only does she support with her prayer, but she is genuinely interested in the details. The other day she stopped me to ask for an update on the progress of my internet books. This was so amazing to me because she is not into this technical world at all, but here she wanted to know how it was working for me. For a second, I hardly knew how to begin answering. Her interest was not just on the surface. Really, I should not have been surprised because in every way we are partners. I try To show the same kind of interest in her projects. This is how God has continued to bless us. We take the three-fold cord found in Ecclesiastes 4:12 very seriously.

Roy and Della started a grocery and notions business. They tested the market and discovered that in this particular community there was a great need. They found a good spot to settle the business. Almost as soon as they opened their doors folks began piling in. After several weeks Roy wanted to give off the look of success. *"Let's spend some of the money so that the neighborhood folks can see that we are about business."* Della did not agree. In fact, her idea was that they change up the inventory and create more of a Gourmet Shoppe. Neither of them could agree with the other so they began traveling separate paths. Della began ordering items that departed from the neighborhood needs and desires. Roy purchased a new wardrobe to create his new image. Soon the business fell into serious decline. People were not getting just what they wanted anymore, so the inventory began backing up. Roy's clothing investments served up another hit on their budget.

The problems with this couple were many. First of all, they did not respect each other's talents and abilities. Next, they refused to compromise. Add to the flaws above the fact that they did not even feel the need to listen to each other. Soon Della became so fed up with the situation that she just wanted out; out of the business, and out of the marriage! We see that this troubled business partnership was only a reflection of what was going on in the marriage relationship. It was far deeper than gourmet foods and fancy wardrobes. They refused to work anything out.

Good partners respect the talents and abilities of each other. They look for ways to include the strengths of their partners in the presentation of the product. Recently I attended a lecture where the presenter was sharing some salient points on handling money. The crowd was very enthusiastic. After the meeting the person who had invited me pointed out that the gentleman making the speech was actually one of the company's founders. What interested me more was that several of the enthusiastic audience members were actually co-founders. They were all equal partners. There they were, cheering on one of the partners as if they were hearing his revelations for the first time. They were all into his presentation. They respected his talents!

To respect is to value. When partners feel that the contribution of a partner is less than valuable the level of overall respect diminishes. When this diminished state is sustained for any length of time a serious restlessness is to be expected. When business partners get to such a sustained state they've got to sit down and regroup. Perhaps certain actions and reactions need to be questioned and explained. It all needs to be placed on the table in order to develop a restoration plan. One partner may have to confess, *"Okay I didn't take the time to see that my behavior was leading us to this or that position or condition,"* or, *"I was careless,* or *"I was insensitive,* (or even*) "I was selfish at that point."* The other partner must at this juncture accept that amends have been instituted and there is now the need to pick up and go from there. It is crucial for these business partners to remember that in the beginning they recognized their individual strengths. The business was built on these strengths. Now even though there has been a hitch in the production as long as there is still the commitment to honor the earlier agreement they can move on. All parties must admit that there have been some missteps that can and will be corrected. The dream can be reconciled.

I listened to a husband/wife team on a Family Life Today radio program. They recommended that husbands and wives could benefit greatly by drafting a working mission statement. Their proposal included regular sessions of examination and evaluation to see if they were on target. This might not work for every couple but developing some system of keeping focused is good.

Marriage partners who find their plan is off target can certainly benefit from some serious sit-down sessions. One of the key and most troublesome elements in marriage is communication. Communication needs to be relentless and ongoing. Relentless and ongoing sound like the same thing however, when I say, *"relentless"*, I mean that dialogue must continue without stopping. When I say, *"ongoing"*, I am referring to the need to not only dialogue but to continually update throughout the journey. Partners producing a product must learn to constantly update and reanalyze the production of that product. Some say that companies like Underwood and Royal the typewriter giants would still be in that kind of business if they had realized the potential of the computer. They had a good product going but failed to keep step with a growing technology. The industry had changed and was moving on.

Reevaluation is an ongoing process. We *should not be reevaluating whether the marriage should or should not go on,* but rather what should the product of the marriage be? *"Is our product where we want it to be? Are we producing the very best that we can produce? And most of all, is God pleased with our product"?*

Another concern that should be mentioned is that of giving time to produce. Sometimes, in order to get the product out and moving the quality/

quantity of the thing is squeezed into a hurried position. Sometimes couples overlook the fact that it takes time and great resources in order to reach the desired outcome. There have been instances where big companies sensed the competition in their field and sought to meet a new demand by rushing through to make a showing. However instead of making a positive splash in the market their rush presented a dud. A little more time, a little more patience, a little more research would have produced a significant and timely product. Instead, what was offered turned out to be less than welcomed.

So, married partners need to take the proper time and patience to produce their very best. If they set out on a journey it would be prudent for them to do everything needed including giving it time. We say that Rome was not built in a day. But when it comes to progress there is a tendency to push our dreams at untenable speeds.

Roy and Della had a dream but their impatience and carelessness push them in uncertain directions. They lost sight of their dream. They stopped supporting each other as they rushed to failure.

Marriage partners must be on one accord intimately

One of the things that so many married couples neglect is the dating scene. Love demands together time. Dating was so important in the beginning of the relationship, why then have some couples allowed it to take on such an unimportant role later in their marriages? Who said that it should be placed down the line because of the other ongoing factors of a busy marriage? It is just as important as it ever was in the beginning. In fact, it is more important now! Dr. Ed Wheat in his list of five Greek words that are used to describe our one English word, "love", uses Eros', the practice of romance. In spite of your business, the number of children you have, time restraints and all of that, you need to take time to date. Even with your busy life-style, you should try to have a date at least every 2 weeks.

Recently, I observed a couple at our church. I know that they often go to an early breakfast on Sunday mornings before church, but this Sunday I came across them sitting in the church dining room, lights out, just sitting and having coffee together. How very wonderful I thought to myself; although they've been married many years with two children, one of them is a baby, they have not succumbed to being too busy to take time to love each other.

I was thinking about these strange times that we have been facing this Covid-19 Pandemic. Most people have been quarantining. I hear a lot of complaining about spouses needing to get away from each other. Really, **it all starts in the mind.** Remember I pointed out in an earlier chapter that **the heart will follow what the mind has chosen to do.** Determine to use the time in positive ways. Build your romance using the extra time you have. We do not have to go out of the house to create a memorable date. Play games, watch films, take bubble baths, candle-light snacks, etc. are just a few ideas. I'm sure you will think of other romantic possibilities once you *decide to explore your positive creativity center.* **That's your wonderful mind!**

Partners must compromise their positions from time to time. Roy and Della each wanted their own way. No compromise was in their will. When they decided that there would be no compromise they also decided that any communication between them was now obsolete. *"There is nothing to talk about,"* Della said. *"Roy wants his own way; he's wrong and I'm not wasting my breath." "To try to talk to that woman is to waste precious time and energy,"* Roy reported. Good partners listen to each other and try to see what will work best for their product. While engaged in a book signing from our first book I met Jackie. She told me that she and her husband were business partners in a land title company. She said that they had learned the importance of compromise both in their business and in their marriage. She said that she was leaving this conference a day early in order to get home so that her husband could attend a conference that was important to him. *"We are partners and make decisions based on* *what is best for our common good."* In a sidesplitting remark she went on to say that, *"Eight years ago when we married I told him I was his wife and that he was stuck with me for life;"* adding, *"So I told him don't let me have to kill you to make this marriage contract work."* Again, **good partners listen to each other** and try to see what will work best for their product. It's not about the individual; it's about the product. You must be willing to communicate and compromise when needed. Ego cannot be allowed to be a factor. There's a joke that makes this point. Once two men climbed some stairs to enter into the town's courthouse. The older man was the senior partner in a prestigious law firm. The young man with him was a junior partner in that same firm. *"Sir I think we ought to go through the rear door,"* said the younger lawyer. *"No, I will not be going through any rear door. When you have worked like I have all these years you have earned the right to go proudly through the main door,"* protested the older gentleman. *"But Sir,"* the young man tried to plead, while stopping short at the landing to the entrance watching wide-eyed as the older self-absorbed man plunged on right into a pan of paint as he opened the door. The junior partner didn't have the years of experience or the reputation of the senior partner but he did read the sign and believed.

Knowing when to compromise is crucial to maintaining a partnership. I recall something else Jackie had to say about her marriage. *"My husband and I are not only business partners but marriage partners as well. We see each other everyday almost 24 hours times seven, every week. People ask me how can I stand it? I tell them that I compartmentalize. I separate what I do at home from the office. When I am at home, I want to be the best homemaker I can be. At work I'm the best there also. I don't mix the two."* Now this is their formula. It may work differently for others. The fact is that each couple has to figure out what works best for them. But they must support each other!

Knowing when to compromise is not at all losing, but rather choosing the best route to achieve the highest result. I've known couples pursuing different personal careers that came together and decided that it was best for them to place one goal on hold in order to advance the other. This is often a tough decision to make.

Kyle dropped out of a promising career in computer technology to accompany his wife to a small-town university to get a graduate degree in dramatic arts. He chose to work in a factory job paying barely over minimum wages in order to provide a steady income. He was greatly overqualified having an MBA in computer science but where they lived there were no job opportunities in his field. He chose to support her dream as part of their overall dream. When Patricia graduated, they moved to an area where he could then pick up where he had paused. She found a faculty position in an arts college and began to earn stable money while he finished up his training and began building the computer business that he had been dreaming of.

Partnership also calls for flexibility. No one is going to do everything the same way. Partnership takes into account that from time to time many little things and perhaps a good deal of the larger things will be done or viewed differently. I laugh to myself that both my wife and I put the toilet paper roll on so that the paper comes over the top. This of course is the correct way to do it (*smile*). But what if one of us, as is often found in couples who are opposites, believed it should be the other way. The important thing is to make sure it is on the shopping list. Small stuff like that drives some people nuts. I'm sure that untold couples argue over which end to squeeze the toothpaste from, or toilet seat up, or toilet seat down?

Again, partners have to be willing to be flexible. In our home we have another interesting situation. I am a professional artist. This makes me want to be real involved in the design and decoration of our home. This may not really bother most men. I have friends who pretty much hand this task over to their wives along with the checkbook and go play golf. Most women I would think, are pretty interested in designing, or having their personal space designed like they want it. My wife encourages me to work out my creations, usually with her putting on the finishing touches. I think that she feels it's like hiring an interior designer and not having to sign his paycheck at the end. Most of the time before beginning I try to explore her mind and heart to get a sense of where she is. Then I try to interpret it through my creative juices. This works extremely well for us.

You know I almost forgot **one very important element of Partnership is humor!** Healthy marriages seem to be marriages filled with times of laughter and lighthearted moments. Honestly my wife makes me laugh, although she would probably suggest that I'm the clown. When things get tense a good old belly laugh is invaluable. In fact, the Bible says that laughter does us good like a medicine (Proverbs17: 22). Life offers us so many moments to share laughter. Seize every one of them, embracing them for all they are worth. They can become like a treasure chest of past memories. We still laugh about one odd event in our first month of being married. During one of those heated moments of passion, she sat straight up in bed and said, "Honey did you put the soda in the refrigerator?" Well, we just laughed and laughed. It was so out of place, so ill-timed but what a wonderful source of humor. We laughed then and it still brings on great laughter now, many decades later.

If you seek them, there are so many moments of life that provide humor. Another golden oldie that causes us to crack up is about me finding this great bargain. Again, it was during the first months of marriage. We were food shopping in a place that was like an early version of Wal-Mart. The name of the place escapes me. But just as most young couples do, we were scrimping to save pennies. I discovered a great deal on some socks. It was a bundle of three pairs of socks for about a dollar. *"Wow I need some socks,"* I said. The price was great so I decided to buy them. I was so grateful because It didn't destroy our meager budget. Later when I got ready to put the first pair on we discovered that the feet of both of the socks had been sewn together somewhere below the ankles and above the toes. It was sort of like the old college prank of short sheeting the bed. I had been short socked! Well, there was no stopping my wife. The girl just lost it. It got worse when I opened the second pair. We found that it had been seamed down the inside panel from top to bottom. I don't know what the third pair looked like but I'm sure that it was just as much of a disaster. We still laugh at my bargain sock buying today.

When you take life and yourself too seriously it dulls the recognition of life's opportunities to laugh. I don't mind laughing at myself. I delight in my wife laughing at me. Her laughter is never ridiculing or demeaning. Together we enjoy the freedom of humor and the healing medicine that it brings. Someone once said, *"A laugh a day keeps the doldrums away!"*

At the time of release, we are simultaneously releasing an additional book, **Parenting:** *equipping Babies for a lifetime.*

We believe that biblical principles always work. We also know that one's culture, tradition and maybe sometimes a particular lifestyle, that some principles are more adaptable than others. It may take a longer time to understand the application. Remember however, some flexibility, does not mean avoiding, ignoring, or rejecting a principle. Godly principles do work!

Please enjoy this latest effort; it is intended to be simple and easy to understand, yet yielding an impactful surge in your relationship energy. Knowledge is power. Power to understand, and power to activate that understanding. Practicing these truths will lead to a greater life. Once again, *I give to you over fifty years of experience and passionate study.*